The Children
of Enoch

Reaping Sorrows

A Shane Moore Presents Release

Edward Gehlert

Genre: Horror / Series
ISBN: 978-1-63196-028-4
First Edition.
Printed in the United States of America.

This is for Mary McDowell. You taught me writing was art. I hope you are proud of the museums I am filling.

CONTENTS

Praise for *Children of Enoch: Reaping Sorrows*

"Gehlert takes a dark world and manages to cloak it in even deeper shadows. *Children of Enoch: Reaping Sorrows* is a must read for fans of *The Apocalypse of Enoch* series."

- Shane Moore, Best Selling Author
of *The Apocalypse of Enoch* series

"After reading Edward Gehlert's books, I have come to one conclusion: The word 'read' doesn't quite cut it. This author scares you shitless with a nightmare on paper. He makes you feel the anguish of his characters. Characters in grisly, violent situations, but yet, in places so familiar you'll be peeking out of your window to make sure that what you're experiencing is definitely just a book, and not an eyewitness account of what could possibly be taking place down the street. You don't 'read' his books… You experience them! A riveting, uneasy, goosebump inducing, guiltily pleasurable experience… But, aren't those the best kind?"

-Brandon Shaw, Co-Host
of *ABC radio's Brothers on Whatever* show

"Edward Gehlert is a wonderful author who knows exactly how to pull you into the story. He knows how to press all your buttons. He's proven that he can scare the shit out of you. Do yourself a favor and read this book. If you're going to have nightmares, you might as well make them worthy of your time and attention."

-Sam Rikard, Author
of *Forge of Feasts and The Wererat's Tale* series

"With his *Children of Enoch* series, Gehlert displays a talent for launching his readers into a world that is both instantly recognizable and thus that much more terrifying. You've been to these places. You know these people. *Reaping Sorrows* puts you on the ropes and keeps you there, with an infectious pace that elevates the danger and desperation of its characters."

-Ryan Colvard, Lead Singer *Big Damn Heroes*

FOREWORD

Every now and then a person comes into your life and simply changes everything about your existence. In some instances these emotions are linked to love. At other times it's the bond of a kindred spirit. But always, it's a sign of growing. We have to grow in order to accommodate new people in our lives. If we remained the same, we'd never evolve into who we are, or who we're supposed to become.

Ed Gehlert had this effect on me. I can't recall exactly how many years I've known him now, but it feels like a lifetime. Between him and his lovely wife, Eva, I've felt at home every time I've been around them. So as you can imagine, when Ed asked me to write the foreword for this book, I took it as a great honor.

From the moment I was introduced to Ed, he made an impression that I could only hope to make on others. He always spoke in an elegant manner, addressing me as "Sir" and carried himself in an educated and respectful presence. Truth be told, the first time he called me "Sir" my mind ran back to my time in the Army. That old expression, 'I work for a living!' jumped into my head, but I'd spent enough time out, I didn't tarnish a fine and proper meeting with a simple jest. Of course, knowing him the way I do now, he would have more than likely followed suit and we would still have gotten on just fine. But there was no need to take a risk on a newly formed business relationship.

In the years that followed I can say from personal experience that Ed has done his very best in every situation I've seen him in. He'll break his back for others, and ask nothing in return. This is a notion I've found myself in more times than I can count and I was proud to see there were others of a like mind. It's one thing to manage a business relationship. It's quite another to manage a personal one. And it takes a true artist to handle them both at the same time. Yet Ed has managed to do this in every aspect of his life. I'm proud to know him. I'm grateful to have him and a colleague. I'm happy to call him friend.

But enough of this mushy stuff. You guys aren't here to read how great of a person the author of this book is. You're here for entertainment. And entertainment is what you'll get. I had the pleasure of reading this book and I can tell you, you're in for a treat. The characters spring to life as soon as you meet them. The story has an air of shadow hanging at the edge of your mind's eye from the very beginning. You'll be gripping the edge of your seat, ready for the monsters to jump out at you, only to realize you're all alone. Of course, it's all an illusion. The moment you let your guard down, they'll spring out in full force; distracting you from the reality that is your life and pulling you head long into the horror that is the *Children of Enoch* series. But never fear, it's only a book. Ed isn't so conniving that he would intentionally hide any ritual spellwork in the pages. He knows the penalties of sucking his readers into his work, never to be heard from again... But maybe that explains why their numbers are always needing to be replenished. I've changed my stance. Use caution, dear reader, for he may have done just that. If you want to be pulled into this book, continue on. If not back away slowly, and never look back. You hold in your hand the best work of Edward Gehlert, at least until his next book. Handle with caution.

-Samuel Rikard
January 2017

PROLOGUE

The aged preacher looked down at the terrified man stretched out on the simple wooden bed. Concern was etched in the lines on the holy man's face. His knuckles had turned white from grasping the suitcase handle he held in front of him. His frown and the back and forth motion of his jaw as he chewed his lower lip was a clear indication that all was not going as well as he had hoped.

His acolytes were both much younger blue-eyed and blonde-haired women. They shifted on their sock-covered feet as they again checked the handcuffs that held the helpless prisoner up in a half sitting position on the bed. The youngest lady playfully ran her nails down the man's bare chest and tickled his belly before securing the leather strap across his thighs.

Her sister's face tightened into a grimace when she looked at her. The younger woman quickly shot a glance in the pastor's direction to see if he had noticed her touching the prisoner. She breathed a sigh of relief when she noted his eyes were closed and his mouth was moving in silent prayer.

She continued strapping the old leather belts in place, making sure that they were as tight as they would go. Each time she slid a new one into position, the helpless man would moan in pain and try to scream through the gag in his mouth. When she had the last restraint on him she nodded toward her sister.

"Brother Abel, the heretic is ready!" Her sweet voice sounded out of place in the dank cellar of the old farm house.

The preacher's eyes flew open at the pronouncement and he stopped his mumbled prayers. Brother Abel smiled at Susan, the youngest of the women, and softly patted her shoulder. His black cassock rustled gently as he stepped past her to tower over the intruder.

His eyes never left the man's face as his calm voice filled the room. "Thank you, Sister Martha and thank you, Sister Susan. Your service during these trying times will not be forgotten by me. I dare say the whole community is in yer' debt fer' yer' assistance in finding this thieving heretic wanderin' on our lands."

Susan and Martha exchanged worried looks. Martha had seen many things happen in this old cellar over the last few months. None of them had been pleasant. Susan had been spared witnessing any of the atrocities due to her age, but when she turned sixteen a few weeks ago Martha knew it was only a matter of time.

"Did you combine the holy ingredients as I instructed you?" Brother

Abel's voice drew her from those dark thoughts.

"I did as you instructed, Brother Abel." *I don't know what's so fucking holy about antacids and milk you crazy fuck!*

The pastor nodded absently at her and set his suitcase on the man's stomach. He opened it with a casual flip of his hands and started removing items and setting them on a small table next to the headboard of the bed. A cut-off garden hose attached to a funnel, an unopened bottle of olive oil, and a wooden container the size of a large shoe box.

"Sister Martha, if ya' would be so kind as ta' remove the heretic's gag we will now try ta' draw the light of truth from him while we cleanse his soul of sin," Brother Abel whispered as he opened the olive oil.

Martha slowly removed the gag from the terrified man. Sweat had formed in thick pools on his brow and it ran into his eyes causing him to rapidly blink away the stinging sensation. On impulse she wiped the rag she had just taken from his mouth across his forehead.

The back of Brother Abel's hand landed brutally on the side of her head. She stumbled back and nearly fell over, only managing to catch her balance on the footboard of the bed. Tears began forming as she looked at Brother Abel through hate filled eyes. His back was still to her. Susan was shaking in fear and rocking back and forth on shaking legs.

"Forgive me! I had a moment of weakness," Martha spat. "It won't happen again."

"I didn't do anything!" wailed the man on the bed. "Let me go! Please, please oh fuckin' Christ let me GO!"

Brother Abel leaned over and gently, almost lovingly, stroked the man's hair. His touch sent him into wild jerking motions, which drew a chuckle from the holy man.

"I'm gonna ask ya' some questions," began the preacher, "and when I'm satisfied you've told me the truth. I'll let ya' go."

The scared man was furiously nodding his head while Brother Abel spoke. His eyes darted at the three people hovering over him. "I'll tell ya' anything ya' wanna' know!"

The preacher held his hand out toward Martha. "Give me the holy elixir!"

Martha was still a bit unsteady from the blow. She stumbled to a small chest of drawers and opened one. She retrieved five bright stainless steel flasks and handed one to the priest. He reached out and rested his spare hand on her cheek just below where he had struck her.

"Thank you again for your service, Sister Martha. Remember, we are living in a time of trouble and tribulation. We can't show weakness! Everyone left on Earth has sins. Deep, dark sins that are so unforgivable that the Lord Almighty abandoned us. We are left ta' find our own path to righteousness."

Martha did good by only recoiling a little from his touch. Her sister had stopped rocking and was now intently watching what played out between the two of them.

Brother Abel unscrewed the lid of the flask and held it up to their prisoner's mouth. The man had been without food and water for three days, just as he had ordered. The smell of milk coming from the container was too much for him and all caution was ignored as he slurped the thick liquid down.

After the flask was empty, Brother Abel cast it on the ground next to him. "What is your name?"

"I'm Tom McKannon. I'm from Wichita," he blubbered.

Brother Abel smacked Tom across the face. The man stared up at him in shock and wailed, "I answered you! Why'd ya' hit me?"

Brother Abel leaned in closer to him. "Just to give ya' incentive for continued truth. If I think yer' lyin' it'll be much worse. Do ya' believe me?"

"Yes," whined Tom as tears rolled down his face.

"Now, do ya' have ah' family?"

"I was married, but we got a divorce. I cheated on her and left her and the kids for another woman."

Brother Abel's eyes flashed with anger for a moment. "Where is this woman now?"

Tom choked back on his reply. He weighed the possible consequences of his response a few seconds before he answered. "She's waitin' fer' me outside of town. In a big blue barn that has dried wheat fields aroun' it."

Brother Abel smiled while unscrewing the lid to another

flask Martha handed him. He poured the contents down Tom's throat.

"Were ya' married to yer' wife in a church? Did ya' speak holy vows to her?"

"Yes," Tom mumbled while licking his lips.

The preacher opened another flask as he spoke and Tom drank long and deep from it. His stomach was feeling a little odd, but after not eating or drinking for a few days he figured it was just the milk. It didn't taste spoiled to him, but it did have an odd texture and aftertaste he couldn't put his finger on.

"Sister Susan, would ya' step outside and bring in that sack?"

Susan jumped at his command and headed up the stairs leading to the outside of the cellar on the side of the house.

"Tom, I appreciate ya' bein' honest here. It takes a big man ta' confess his sins."

Tom could only manage to nod his head as a response. Brother Abel opened another flask and poured it down his prisoner's throat. Tom choked for a few seconds and the preacher's eyes went wide. Brother Abel let out a slow breath when the man's coughing stopped.

"Last night I prayed long an' hard about ya'. I prayed ta' all the powers that be about how we could help ya'."

Brother Abel was momentarily interrupted as the cellar door opened and Susan ambled down the stairs. Her delicate hands hefting a brown, burlap sack. She was expressionless and her eyes looked dull and vacant. After placing the sack next to Brother Abel she backed away.

"Well, you'll be happy ta' know they answered me. They told me that we had ta' free ya' of yer' burden of sin. They told me where yer' harlot was a' hidin' and that we should go get 'er."

Tom's face paled. He sucked in air as his eyes widened. Martha stared more closely at the bag on the floor next to the preacher's feet. Part of the sack was stained a darker color. It looked like it might be dried...

Brother Abel moved at blinding speed. He snatched the sack from the ground. Like a macabre magic trick the twisted holy man plucked the severed head of Tom's lover from it. He presented it to him by her golden hair and shook it at him while proclaiming, "The moment of yer' deliverance is at hand, brother!"

Tom screamed in terror at the vacantly staring blue-eyed head while Martha covered her mouth with the back of her right hand. Susan continued to stare dully ahead of her at the wall above the bed.

"Whaaaaaa!" Tom wailed in horror as Brother Abel tossed the gruesome trophy on the bed next to him.

The warped preacher grabbed the olive oil. He straddled the bound man and forced some into his mouth. The helpless man swallowed. He felt it coating the back of his throat. He jerked wildly, doing his best to buck Brother Abel off of him. His bonds proved too tight for any such action to be fruitful.

After a few moments the holy man grabbed the hose and forced it down Tom's throat. It took a few tries before it was properly placed so his airway was unaffected. Tom made gagging noises, but nothing spewed from the funnel that was now connected to his stomach.

Martha was feeling numb as she watched the preacher pour more olive oil in the funnel. Brother Abel climbed off of Tom. He picked up the wooden box and clutched it tightly for a few moments before saying, "It was vermin like you that turned this world in ta' shit! Them powers I've been a' talkin' ta', they told me what I need ta' do ta' cleanse ya'!"

The preacher flung the lid off the box and pulled out a small, white furry mouse by the tail. Without hesitation he dropped it in the funnel and watched it slide down into the blackness of Tom's stomach.

Tom froze. His mind couldn't comprehend everything that was happening. Beth was dead that much he could take in, but not the rest of the hell that was unfolding around him. He remained still like a child hiding under the covers at night just hoping the monsters wouldn't get him; praying that if he didn't move everything would be okay.

That delusion was shattered as the preacher pulled out mouse after mouse and dropped them in the funnel. Tom didn't feel anything at first although he heard squeaks echoing not only from the wooden box being clutched by Brother Abel, but also from the funnel.

It was maybe thirty seconds, twenty-three mice, before he felt them trying to claw and eat their way out of him. He couldn't scream because of the pressure the hose was placing against the inside of his throat. He bucked on the bed and tried twisting in all directions. He pissed himself and sobbed uncontrollably.

Brother Abel stepped away from the bed and set the box gently on the nightstand. The mice had been placed where the voices wanted them. Lifting his head and hands toward the ceiling he began praying. "Oh Those Who Watch take notice of this ritual of purification, may his pain fill yer' vessels with pleasure. I have done what was commanded of me in yer' name!"

Martha finally moved. She ran to the younger woman and held her close. She felt sudden, hot tears streaming from her sister's eyes. Crying, both of them clung to the other. Tom's painful moans and the eerie squeaking of the mice echoing up through the hose and out of the funnel caused both of their legs to buckle. Together they crumpled to the floor and continued sobbing. Each of them let out a wail of fear when they felt the tender hands of Brother Abel grasp their shoulders.

"No need for tears, girls. Those mice are just fine. That's what all those antacids were for."

Susan and Martha looked up at the preacher in shock and disbelief when he continued, "The funnel will keep 'em supplied with air. With any luck, we'll have all our little friends out ah' him in a day or two. Once they get their fill."

THE CHILDREN OF ENOCH

OF ENOCH

REAPING SORROWS

"The one who sows the good seed is the Son of Man. The field is the world, and the good seed is the sons of the kingdom. The weeds are the sons of the evil one, and the enemy who sowed them is the devil. The harvest is the end of the age, and the reapers are angels. Just as the weeds are gathered and burned with fire, so will it be at the end of the age."

Matthew 13:37 - 40

1

IF THAT MOCKINGBIRD DON'T SING

Sweat streamed down his forehead covering the front of his shirt like an exploded water balloon. His hands shook each time he tried to open the lid to his canteen. The muscles in his arms were barely responding to his mental command to twist and pull. When the container finally popped open Justin took a long and well deserved gulp of water.

He let out a groan as he sat on an old fallen log and stretched his legs in front of him. He admired the work he had just completed from his newfound place of comfort and allowed a slight smile to creep to the edges of his mouth. The new wall looked good.

He had started on it a week ago using lumber he had found in one of the storage sheds. He had never built a wall before. Of course in the last few months he had done a lot of things he never even could have imagined doing. Running for his life from zombies was on the top of that list.

His smile quickly faded away. He looked at the wall again,

this time using a more critical eye. It would provide some concealment and cover, but that would be it. *I just wasted a week! Those little creepers can just jump right over that and the big ones...*

Justin threw down his canteen with enough force that it bounced several feet away from him. His face suddenly felt hot. Salty tears mixed with his sweat to form a steady stream falling from his head.

Why did I even bother!

"Justin! Come look at this!"

Sean's voice pulled him away from his frustrations. The former pastor leapt to his feet in panic and looked at the tree line where the yell had come from. He was greeted with the sight of Sean and Elizabeth carrying a full stringer of fish between them. Even from this distance he could tell they were all good size and it was easy to see the smiles of the two kids.

He put his index finger over his mouth. The motion caused the kids to look at each other and then all around them. Even though they hadn't seen any of the demon-spawned brats in a month, everyone knew it wasn't safe to take chances.

Justin looked towards the treehouse where James was busy keeping watch. The older teen looked down at him and just shook his head. The boy's hair was frazzled and unkempt much like his and Sean's. In fact Elizabeth was the only one who still made any effort at grooming.

Watching as the two kids walked slowly across the field Justin could see them whispering to each other and smiling. He was still relieved that the girl had finally woken up.

She had been knocked unconscious during a vicious struggle against the beasts. James and Sean had carried her until they had found Justin, Matt, and Father Murray. Justin stayed with the children while Matt and the priest went to secure transportation for them.

He shuddered as he remembered the horde of creatures that swarmed around the small shed when they had returned with a truck. He could still hear Matt screaming at them to stay inside while his friend and Father Murray sped off into the night, leading the hellish children away.

That was two months ago and the last time he saw his best

friend. Justin understood that more than likely both of them had been killed and eaten. It made him furious at himself for being such a helpless drunkard when Matt needed him the most. It made him hate himself in ways he never thought possible.

He watched as Sean and Elizabeth entered the small compound and placed the stringer of fish in a metal water trough. The splashing of the helpless creatures as they tried in vain to escape their fate made the former pastor wince. It seemed like they had too much in common with his own predicament. The two kids were smiling at each other and talking in low tones as they walked into the shed where the butchering tools were stored.

"She gets better each day."

Justin turned towards James who had climbed down from his lookout perch and smiled. "That she does. I honestly didn't think she'd make it after being out for four days. It still amazes me she doesn't have brain damage."

"She's in love with Sean. That screams 'brain damage' to me," joked James.

Justin snorted out a short burst of laughter. He hadn't allowed himself the luxury of mirth in a long time and it felt good.

"Falling in love with him is normal. If she was in love with you then I'd worry."

James was shocked by the joke. He hadn't heard Justin make any attempt at humor since all of this started. He smiled at the former pastor.

They looked at each other for a moment. A broken down drunkard and a boy who would never know what a normal childhood was like. Their smiles faded at the same time. As if each one suddenly felt guilty about having the audacity to be happy.

"When are you going to stretch the barbed wire over the top?" the boy asked.

Justin looked at the new wall. It connected two small outbuildings together and cut off line of sight into the rest of the camp. He sighed. "I think we can save the wire for something else."

"Bonjour," came a soft call from around the edge of the larger storage unit. "Est-ce que quelqu'un me comprendre encore?"

James rolled his eyes when he heard Firmin's voice and headed back up the tree as Justin turned around to communicate with the displaced Frenchman.

"Firmin," Justin smiled. "As soon as we find an English to French dictionary you and I are going to drink ourselves stupid!"

The foreigner creased his brow in frustration and fought back the urge to scream. He had been unlucky enough to be part of a cross-country tour group filled with European visitors when the creatures began their rampage a few months ago. After the bus had been ripped apart by one of those... THINGS... he had found himself running alone through the woods followed by the hellish screams of the dying.

He had managed to scavenge barely enough food from abandoned houses to live on. After a month and a half he had reconciled himself to the fact he was going to be dead soon. Luckily Sean had found him sleeping in a small clearing close to their camp and led him in. He was so thrilled to be around other people at first that he didn't mind they couldn't understand him or that everything out of their mouths was gibberish. Now here he was, hot and miserable in mid-August and the lack of knowing anything was finally taking its toll on him.

Firmin nodded his head at the former pastor and watched as the fish splashed in the trough. He glanced up when he heard the creak of a door. He watched as the two young love birds walked toward him and Justin. Both of them held knives in their hands. The blades gleamed in the morning sunshine.

"Pour être jeune à nouveau," the Frenchman greeted them with a small smile.

"Hello, Firmin," both the children responded.

"Justin," Elizabeth began, "do you think it's okay to check the traps today after we clean these fish?"

Justin bit his lower lip and wrinkled his face in thought. Things had been quiet lately and the traps were only a half mile away from the camp. He looked at Sean and nodded.

"Make sure you both take a gun with you. Izzy, grab the .22 pistol and I want Sean to take one of the shotguns."

"I still have my 9 mm, Justin. That should be good enough."

"Don't argue with him, boy."

Everyone spun around to face the edge of the clearing where the voice sounded from. A camouflage-wearing man was walking toward them. The old man had a brushy, unkempt beard and a rifle slung over his left shoulder. They collectively breathed a sigh of relief when they recognized Mark.

Mark had been a friend of Clyde's and had showed up at the small compound the day after Justin and the kids arrived. The former pastor had met him on several occasions. Even though they were not close each understood that the other was well respected in Clyde's eye and that meant they could trust each other.

"I wasn't arguing!" Sean huffed.

Mark ignored the kid and motioned for Justin to follow him. "We need to talk."

The experienced survivalist had been gone for a week on a self-imposed scouting mission. The look on his face left no room to question whether or not his statement was a request. Justin followed Mark into Clyde and Emma's former residence; a nice log home with a loft and wood stove. Mark primed the pump on the sink in the kitchen and drew a large glass of water.

Even though he was pushing sixty-four the older man was in much better shape than Justin ever could remember being. Justin waited patiently while Mark took a few drinks. The man's slender frame slowly sank onto a chair next to the table and he stared at Justin as if wondering how to start the conversation.

"It wasn't good, was it?"

"What do ya' mean, Pastor?"

Justin winced slightly at the title. "Whatever you saw. It wasn't good was it?"

Mark took another drink of water and then rested the cup between his hands on the table, rolling it back and forth in his palms.

"A couple weeks back during one of the bad nights ya' had

you said something about how this was all God's doing. How we missed our golden ticket to the Rapture and now we had to pay for our sins. Do you remember that, Pastor?"

Justin's face was red with embarrassment. The 'bad night' the old man was talking about was when he had found a stash of alcohol and had proceeded to get rip roaring drunk.

"Stop calling me 'Pastor' and, yes, I remember the night. What about it?"

"I think you were right."

Justin's growing anger fled from him like a frightened child. He felt the hairs on the back of his neck raise and a chill went through him. The look in Mark's eyes told him that no joke was being made.

"What did you see?" The former holy man asked.

"Rosebud is gone. All the buildings have been burned beyond use from what I could tell. Owensville, well, the same story there. Gerald has a few places still standing, but a bunch of those fuckin' monsters are roaming the streets."

Justin felt a sinking feeling in his stomach as Mark continued, "I came across a group of eighteen people. They were camped north of Owensville just off Highway 19. One of them was acting funny. He kept giggling now and then, like he was off his rocker."

Mark took another drink of water and gulped it down. "The other people kept telling him to keep quiet, but he just got louder and louder. Finally, they gagged him and tied him up. I got in real close and heard them talking. It seems their friend had been in a bad scrape with one of those little demonic bastards. He came out of it with a few scratches, lucky him."

"So you think his mind just snapped?"

Mark shook his head and held up his hand for Justin to be quiet. "No. After an hour he got real still. One of them got up close to check on him and then…"

The old man shuddered and drained his glass. "He broke clean through the leather belts that held his arms and grabbed one of those other fella's heads and twisted it backwards. Things got real messy after that. He kept fighting and laughing. Those… giggles. I'll never forget 'em! He sounded happy about what he was doing. He killed five of those poor bastards and hurt one's ankle pretty bad. Then some fella' dressed like a priest shot him in the —"

"Priest?" Justin leaned forward.

"Yeah, some priest shot the thing in the head with a pistol and it went down. The rest of the bunch helped that one fella' up and they gathered their gear and scooted out of there in under an hour."

Justin's mind was reeling. *If that was Father Murray then he would know what happened to Matt!* "Was this priest kinda' young? Like around my age?

"Forget the goddamned priest for one fuckin' second! After they left I saw some kind of dark smoke coming out of the mouth of that dead body. It was black as night and it faded away into the ground. That ain't natural, none of this is I know… but THAT especially! Somethin' evil, somethin' from Hell, is here on Earth and it wants us all dead!"

Mark was shaking as he finished. "That's when I made my way back here."

Justin digested what Mark had just told him. He knew that biblical things had come to pass. He knew that this was just the start to the end of the world. He knew he had to find Matt.

"Where was this group at?"

"Up Highway 19 toward Cuba, next to Bem Church Road. They took off down the gravel."

The screams of Anna spurred him on to speeds greater than he ever believed possible. Mercifully those screams were abruptly cut short. He was thankful for that. He was also thankful that he hadn't been a target during the ambush by the clever little creepers.

Luke dared a look behind him as he ran. A mob of the beasts slinked around the bodies of his sisters, fighting each other over their flesh. One of the grey skinned creatures ripped Clair's head off of her torso before he could avert his gaze.

Luke ran on fighting down tears and the urge to vomit. He ran until he felt his lungs burning. Then he ran some more. He ran until his bare feet were bleeding, leaving a crimson trail for anyone, or anything, to follow. Then he ran some more. He ran until his vision clouded over and the ringing in his ears sounded like the roar of cannons. He slipped on something and felt himself falling, but the ground never caught him...

He awoke sometime during the early morning hours to a dog licking the bottom of his left foot. He opened his eyes, but couldn't remember why he was laying in the middle of the road. He stared up at the night sky and could no longer hold back his tears as his memory returned and the reality of this new world overcame him.

They exploded from him in great bouts. Long mournful sobs echoed through the wilderness on each side of him. He cried, even as the rough tongue of the dog moved to his other foot. His dad had told him once that a dog licking a wound would help it heal, but he didn't know how much truth was in that.

A thought came to him. *How can an animal that eats its own shit have a healthy mouth?*

The thought of that suddenly repulsed him and he jerked his leg up and away from the animal. He was too surprised to even scream when he suddenly felt claws dig into his leg as it was pulled back down accompanied by a deep growl.

For the first time since he opened his eyes he took in his surroundings. Down at his feet was a lone creeper. Its grey mottled skin absorbing much more daylight than it was reflecting. He began to shake as a wave of panic flooded his body.

The monster continued to lick the bottom of his foot. It's rough tongue slowly peeling skin away from him, causing blood to flow again. The creature moaned softly as it tasted the warm liquid and began to lick even harder.

It's treating me like a fucking lollipop! I'm nothing more than a goddamned fleshsicle for this thing!

He tensed his body and prepared to use the last bit of his strength to kick the child-beast. Flexing his muscles he sent his leg as hard as he could against the side of its head. The blow landed solidly and the creeper was flung off him.

He started to scamper to his feet, but the demon was on him faster than he could imagine. It rammed him face down onto the hard pavement and howled in his ear. Luke closed his eyes and silently pleaded to whatever goodness remained in the world for a fast death.

CRACK! The noise startled him. He felt the monster stiffen for a brief moment and then it toppled off of him. Luke rolled over on his back and pulled himself into a sitting position. Blood from his freshly busted forehead ran down his face.

Turning his head to the left he saw a figure emerging from the woods on the side of the road. As the stranger steeped into the moonlight Luke's face cracked into the first smile he had in over a month. Coming toward him was a priest carrying a pistol.

"Thank you! God… Thank you! I was sure I was dead but now—"

CRACK! The same noise that saved him heralded the end of Luke's life. Father Murray slowly lowered the weapon while stepping in closer to make sure he had hit the kid in the head.

"What the fuck!"

Thomas sighed and turned to face Matt. "He was bitten. You know what happens."

"He's just a fucking kid! I didn't see the damn thing bite him! Why'd you kill him?!" Matt screamed as he limped from the woods on a makeshift crutch.

The priest pointed at the corpse's feet. "The monster was licking him so hard he was bleeding. Saliva and blood, bite or not, that thing's fluids were mixed with his."

"We don't know if that's how it works," Matt grunted. "We don't know how any of this works!"

"I know that when we tried to save Jacob all it took was the thing drooling in his mouth!" Thomas shot back, "Do you really want to argue about this out here?"

Matt glared at the priest, but kept silent. Bending over he examined the teenagers feet. The creature's spittle was all over them. Matt straightened himself and looked the body up and down a few times.

"Are you ready to get back yet?" Thomas asked with a smirk as he casually strolled towards the woods.

Matt looked from the body at his feet to the monster retreating in front of him. He briefly entertained the thought of clubbing him to death with his crutch.

"Sorry, kid," he murmured as he followed Father Murray. "I have a feeling that bastard actually did you a favor."

He was awakened by the sound of shattering glass coming from the kitchen. Before his eyes were even open instinct kicked in and he snatched the hammer from the nightstand. He was rolling out of bed just as one of the devilish beasts crashed against the wall behind him.

Spinning around he led the way with his weapon. He was greeted with a sickening *crunch* as metal connected with bone. Nick felt pieces of meat and other gore splatter over his face as the twisted creature's head caved in from the blow.

His nostrils filled with a stench of what seemed like a hundred matches all being struck at once. His stomach lurched as the odor physically pulled up the contents of his most recent meal. Half-digested cornflakes and beef jerky mixed with bile sprayed across the blood soaked sheets and corpse of the monster. His body convulsed from the sudden explosion of vomit. He briefly collapsed on the side of the bed shaking.

A loud *thump* sounded from the roof and Nick's head jerked upwards. He held his breath watching dust fall from the ceiling as more monsters leapt and shuffled around on the shingles above. He gritted his teeth and clutched the hammer tightly. In a move inspired by sheer desperation or pure brilliance he flung the small nightstand out of the bedroom window and bolted for the kitchen.

Without a second thought he dove through the window that had been destroyed by the monster's entry. Once he hit the ground he sped as fast as he could from the structure. Hissing came from all around him as he twisted his way through thick trees and underbrush. Breathing heavily he cursed the Missouri landscape for being so hilly and uneven. He blindly swung his hammer at anything that got close. More than once he almost stumbled from the force of missed attacks, but every time a blow landed it caused his jaw to clench in satisfaction.

His muscles burned and his movements began to get shaky.

His eyes darted around looking for a place he could make a last stand. Just as he was giving up hope the first rays of dawn lit up a small outcropping of rock. If he could just make it…

His breath was torn from his lungs as he hit the earth. One of the little bastards had ripped his legs out from underneath him. Nick rolled onto his back and swung his hammer. One of the creature's long, spindly arms blocked the blow and it used its other clawed hand to grapple the hammer from him and toss it almost casually several feet behind them.

The demon-spawn's jaws protruded from its face. They were much more canine-like than the once delicate features of a child. It lunged in to bite him. Nick was still fighting for breath. He lurched to the side and managed to fling himself on top of the beast. He held the monster by its yellowish-gray neck with his left hand and used his remaining strength to continually pummel the demon in its maw.

After a few moments, his blows, aided by the heavy leather gloves he wore, had left the fiend's face completely unrecognizable. A sulfuric stench of tainted blood wafted up from the crushed skull making Nick's eyes burn. He staggered to his feet and only made it a few steps before a cascade of rustling leaves and underbrush was joined by a chorus of ghastly hissing.

He slowly turned towards the sounds and was greeted with the sight of four horridly deformed children. The fiends' greyish-mottled skin stretched taut over sunken cheekbones, making their puss-yellow eyes seem bulbous. Cloth hung from their mostly naked bodies in scraps; remnants of the clothing they once wore. His brow creased with determination as sweat poured from his body, warping his hawk-like features into something that would appear menacing if any of the onlookers were still human. He swore under his breath in frustration wishing he could see his hammer.

"Alright ya' fuckin' twats!" He barked, his crisp English accent broken by ragged breathing, "Come on then!" The Brit shrieked as he straightened into his full height of six foot. If the creatures were alarmed by his size they did a good job of hiding it.

The demonic children slinked along the ground. Their

wicked claws cut deep furrows into the terrain and sliced through small roots as they advanced on him. The children's ashen faces twisted in smiles showing razor-sharp teeth glinting from misshapen jaws.

Nick sidled backwards as the aroma of the disturbed earth drifted over him. It reminded him too much of graveyards and funerals; of attending wakes and eating fancy foods as the recently dead started their journey towards eternity. While eyeing the mockeries of children in front of him a nervous laugh escaped his pursed lips. *I won't have a funeral, but they'll enjoy a feast!*

His muscles tensed with the expectation of attack. Sweat poured from his face and his arms shook. He was about to make a suicidal leap at the closest one when his vision suddenly narrowed on his lost hammer. It was behind the group of devil-spawn.

Trying to position a tree between him and the closest beast he lurched to the left as hard as he could. Three of the monsters leapt at him. Two of the creatures collided in mid-air and came crashing down in a flurry of slashes and bites directed at each other. One of the hellish fiends flung an arm out and grasped the branch just above Nick's head. It swung around and landed on its feet clutching the tree trunk for additional support. The remaining monster cackled wildly and bounced back and forth with monkey-like movements keeping Nick in its spiteful gaze as the Brit bounded for the hammer.

He bolted a half-dozen yards toward his weapon. A feeling of overwhelming panic caused him to suddenly surge to his right. The two creatures hot on his heels stumbled over one another as they adjusted their pursuit only narrowly missing their target. Behind them, the other two beasts were still locked in battle. Corrupted blood flowed freely from dozens of wounds on each of the twisted children. Whatever hate, whatever evil that lurked in each of them refused to let the other go.

Diving forward with outstretched arms Nick snatched the hammer from the ground. Rolling as best he could the Brit came up on his knees with the hammer clutched tightly in his shaking right hand. He was ready to take as many of them with him as he could.

The two creatures pursuing him split off. One swerved to his right with the other breaking toward his left side. Nick's mind spun as he took in the situation. It didn't matter which creature he turned to face; it would leave him completely open to attack from the other one. Thankfully the other two monsters were continuing to rip each other to shreds.

Leaping toward the brute on his right the displaced Englishmen put all of his strength into his swing. With a speed he never thought possible the demon-spawn ducked. Nick watched helplessly as his weapon whizzed harmlessly over the monster's head. His momentum spun him to the ground. Before he was able to regain his senses the closest creature was on him.

Seeing razor-like talons tearing into his leather jacket snapped him from his momentary stupor. He lashed out with a blind swing toward the fiend on top of him. The move saved his life. At that moment the other beast was lunging in and received the full force of the impact on its chin.

Clutching its shattered jaw the child-demon lurched to the side and yowled. Bone shards protruded from the creature's cheek and yellowish blood spurted from the jagged rips in its flesh. Pounding on the ground and wailing in pain the beast retreated into the woods.

If the creature on top of Nick had any concern for its hellish companion it didn't show. Monstrous claws slashed down again and again accompanied by gleeful cackling. His jacket absorbed most of the hits, but a few grazes pierced his skin causing burning pain to permeate his chest.

Swinging the hammer at his assailant was proving to be useless. He couldn't get enough force behind the attacks to break through the hell-child's lighting quick parries. Dropping the hammer Nick grabbed the creature's arms. He was awarded only a moment of relief before the demon cackled madly at him and easily broke free of his grasp. The strength of the child was amazing!

The Brit grabbed the monster by its shoulders and tried twisting it off of him while bucking. In retaliation, the beast grabbed his hands and jerked them painfully to the side. Nick was helpless and feeling dizzy. He didn't know if it was from his exertions, loss of blood, or the hopelessness of the world he was now living in.

As his vision was fading he watched as the demon-child slowly leaned toward him with fangs bared. He dimly heard the sound of rushing footsteps approaching. *The other two must have set their differences aside to enjoy some British cuisine.* He chuckled to himself at the thought.

As he was losing consciousness he felt the weight of the creature slide from him. The odor of sulfur exploded all around him. It was so overpowering his mind jolted awake for a brief moment. He looked up.

Standing over him he saw a slender giant wearing chainmail armor. Nick's eyes dully focused on the bloody mace he carried. Tears streamed from behind the young man's glasses and flowed down his cheeks as the weapon fell from shaking hands.

"Ha! Well, this is enough insanity for one day," mumbled the Brit. Nick let his mind fall into the darkness that had been waiting for him.

"Two are better than one, because they have a good return for their work: If one falls down, his friend can help him up. But pity the man who falls and has no one to help him up!"

Ecclesiastes 4:9 -10

CRY BABY BUNTING

The gruesome images that assailed him every time he closed his eyes made thinking with a clear head nearly an impossible task. Ethan had seen things. Things from his most terrifying nightmares had been brought to life. It was this horror that froze him and caused him to only be able to stand by helplessly as people were slaughtered around him like animals.

St. Louis had been a living hell. Dealing with fallout rain from the Callaway Nuclear Plant was bad enough, but dealing with THEM was something else altogether. Ethan fought for control of his shaking hands as his mind conjured up images of the events that had led him back home.

The convention was fun at first. He had met Peter Mayhew, Matt Hill, and a few other heroes of his childhood. He finally found an affordable suit of chainmail and he was parading around in it. He had made some new friends and joined a zombie-fighting cosplay group called Z.O.D. when he found out there was a chapter located in his area.

When hell broke loose Z.O.D. turned in their fake guns for real ones. Some of the members were former military and a few were active police officers. Their training was the only reason why so many made it out of the convention alive. There were about twenty or so of them at first, but as the days and weeks went by that number was brutally whittled down to six. Ethan could still hear their screams when he tried to sleep. He could still see Anna's bright green eyes pleading for him to save her when one of the little bastards ripped her throat out and stole her life. He could hear Brian so steadfast and determined telling him to run while he barred the door to one of the buildings to keep the monsters from following. He ran. He had not seen Brian since.

The country was no better than the city had been. Packs of roaming flesh-crazed monsters were everywhere. The thick woods and underbrush were a perfect place for the clever little ones to hide and they used it to bloody efficiency.

Yesterday he lost his last friend. Benny had managed to shout a warning before the small pack of feral children descended on him. Ethan was lucky enough to be carrying Benny's mace when it happened. Crushing one of the beast's skulls had opened an escape route for him, but not for Benny.

He ran until he collapsed. As he was regaining his strength a strange calmness overcame him. He had been running for months. He wasn't going to run anymore. Ethan backtracked and managed to find the group of hell-spawns. In the early morning light he saw six of the child-monsters creeping up on an old wooden house in the middle of the woods.

Moving toward them he watched as one of the creatures sniffed at a window then leapt through it. Crashing erupted from inside the cabin and four of the remaining children bounded to the roof. The last one scurried toward the rear of the dwelling. Ethan went into motion.

The tumultuous activity inside and on top of the cabin masked his approach. Rounding the corner he saw one grey-mottled beast preparing to crash through a window. Ethan towered over the demon-spawn by a good four feet. He brought the heavy mace down as hard as he could. The blunt edge shattered the tainted skin and bone of the monster at the base of its neck. The force of the blow severed the spinal cord and sent the child's head crashing against the side of the window frame.

Ethan stared at the twitching body as yellowish blood stained the rotting wood of the building. A familiar acrid odor hit him, but couldn't place it. A crashing from the other side of the decrepit house made Ethan whirl around. He took a few paces toward the noise then spun around when he heard crashing coming from the underbrush behind him.

He saw a man wearing a leather jacket fleeing towards the woods. It looked as though the right half of the hair on his head had been ripped away leaving the remaining long bright red locks trailing behind him as he ran. Only four child-beasts were in pursuit. Ethan climbed into the window next to the creature he had killed and took a quick run through the house. He found the fifth monster crumpled on a bed with its head caved in and covered with vomit. Looking out the broken window he was just in time to see the last of the creepers disappearing after the unfortunate man.

The calmness was still with him. Climbing out the window he ran after the hell-beasts. He didn't even feel the encumbrance of his armor until he reached the woods. It seemed as though each limb, each twig, was catching on the metal rings. He was viciously yanked to the ground when the tendril of a branch interlaced itself with his hauberk.

Untangling himself as quietly as possible allowed him to hear thrashing and screeches of joy from the monsters ahead of him. He thought about the stranger and began to rip at his bonds. He wouldn't let anyone else die.

Once freed, he adjusted his glasses and made his way more carefully towards the scuffle; avoiding bushes and underbrush as best he could while letting his long legs carry him forward. The sounds got louder and he could hear grunting. He came into a small clearing and was stunned to see two of the monsters fighting each other. One of the other children was running into the thicker woods. The remaining demon-spawn was on top of the man.

Without thinking Ethan bashed in the skull of one of the beasts. As it toppled over he stomped as hard as he could on the neck of the other one. Gurgling, the demon-child lashed out at his legs with its wicked claws. Ethan felt a moment of disappointment as he watched hundreds of metal rings getting ripped from his armor. His disappointment was wiped away as he stomped on the monsters head again and again. He watched almost distantly as one of the child's eyes burst from its socket.

Hearing a yelp of human pain brought his attention back to the helpless man. Ethan bolted at the unholy beast and swung his mace down with all the force his momentum carried. He felt only the slightest resistance on the handle of his weapon as it pounded the demon's head into its shoulders.

Ethan started shaking. Tears burst from his eyes as the warming feeling of calmness left his body. He had saved one life, but what was that compared to all the lives he had witnessed lost? He looked down at the man he had saved. Their eyes met for an instant and Ethan could see relief and thanks reflected in them. Chuckling, the man murmured something and passed out.

Ethan crumpled next to him. Tears were still streaming down his face. He saw through a misty haze that the stranger was bleeding. Pulling a pocket knife out and lifting up his armor Ethan began cutting scraps from his shirt. He removed the man's jacket as gently as he could and pressed the cloth into the wounds. They seemed to be mostly superficial. Breathing a sigh of relief the young man sat on his knees.

Sniffling back more tears he took in his surroundings. He knew he was somewhere near Owensville, but he wasn't exactly sure how much distance remained. He had kept as close to Highway 50 as he could while still using the terrain to hide. Sometimes he wandered too far and had to retrace his steps, but overall he knew he was making progress.

For the next hour he watched the stranger and cleaned his wounds. Ethan relaxed when the injured man's breathing became regular and strong. He was working out an idea for a makeshift litter when he heard rustling in the underbrush.

They were happy with their catch. Most of the traps had yielded a rabbit or squirrel and that meant fresh meat. Sean would do his best to end the critters lives as painless as he could while Elizabeth looked away. Even though she knew the animals had to die so they could live it still bothered her to kill them. Fish were different. Fish looked so alien to her she had no trouble scaling and filleting them. A rabbit was just too cute for her to bring herself to kill.

That was one of the reasons she liked Sean so much, he was just so practical. He wasn't the cutest boy compared to the others who had made their way out to Clyde's, but there was something different about him. She couldn't even describe to herself what it was. She just knew he was special.

They walked close to one another as they worked their way through the landscape to the final trap. His presence was comforting to her. She knew he wouldn't let anything happen to her. She had heard from James about how Sean saved their lives when everyone woke up a zombie.

Hiding her smile, she glanced back at James. His Z.O.D. dog tags flopping against a camouflage tactical vest he had found at Clyde's made him look almost like a real soldier. No matter how many times people told James the creatures couldn't be zombies it still solicited a vehement response form the kid. He was so adamant in his stance that everyone just started calling them that. If nothing else just so they could avoid an argument with a teenager.

James caught her gaze for a second and winked at her. Feeling her face heat up, she turned away from him and planted her eyes on the ground. She hoped Sean hadn't seen the wink. The less he knew about her history with the other boy the better.

Sean enjoyed the hike. It wasn't too far from their little community, yet far enough out where he didn't have to worry about the looks people gave him. He knew what they were saying behind his back. He knew that rumors were flying about his miraculous recovery at the same time almost everyone else in his class went into comas.

People thought he was only one step away from turning into one of the little demonic creepers himself. He ran his mind over that incident time and time again. He had shyly brought up the subject to Elizabeth a few times. She said that she didn't hear anything or feel anything. She only knew that one second their friends were playing baseball and the next moment they were on the ground. Sean didn't know what to make of it all. He could still almost feel the music flowing through him. He could almost feel it pulling him towards something beautiful.

If he concentrated hard enough on it his head would hurt and his stomach would feel twitchy. It was almost like he was straining his brain to remember a dream. Shaking his thoughts away Sean focused on the task at hand. One more trap and then they could head back to Clyde's.

He adjusted the game bag on his side. The weight of six rabbits and five squirrels had caused it to shift uncomfortably against his leg. He held his hand up for the group to stop. Words had been abandoned once the camp was out of sight. As one they stopped.

Sean unslung the shotgun from his shoulder and unhitched the bag from his belt. The shifting weight caused him to stumble on his feet and he toppled over. A squeak escaped from Elizabeth while James snickered at him. Sean felt a moment of rage building then his jaw suddenly went slack. He felt like ice was running through his veins. Raising his hand he numbly pointed at a small stone cairn a few feet away from them.

James and Elizabeth looked at each other in confusion. Sean had never told them about how he had found his pistol. He had never told them about the mysterious pile he was compelled to sift through when the first night of hell had started. All they could see was that their friend was terrified of a rock pile.

Sean crawled toward the pile on quivering hands and knees. Slowly at first then with an increased fervor he pulled rocks from the pile. He clawed his hands into the dirt. He pulled with all his might. The cairn tumbling down around him, he heard James inhale sharply. Inside the middle of the debris resting on some type of unfamiliar cloth was a small brown bottle of liquid. The label had been destroyed by water seeping through the dirt.

Reaching out Sean snatched it from the cloth. Opening the

lid produced a loud *pop*. He smelled the contents. He gagged at the stench.

"What is it?" whispered James.

Sean shrugged his shoulders and held it out for his friends to smell. They scrunched up their noses at the odor. None of them could place it. Sean carefully replaced the stopper and stood up. Without another word he secured the game bag to his belt and slipped the vial in his pocket.

James and Elizabeth exchanged worried looks as Sean silently walked away from them. They followed closely until James tapped Sean on the shoulder. The younger boy turned around. His face was more composed. James pointed at his own eyes and then in front of the small group. He wanted to scout ahead. Sean gave a quick nod and stood next to Elizabeth as his friend silently crept through the woods.

The young woman slipped her hand into Sean's. He looked at her and smiled. Pulling him close she put her arms around his neck. Sean's breathing quickened as he looked into her eyes. They were a calming mirror amidst the chaos around them and he could lose himself for hours just staring at her beauty. Before he knew what was happening her mouth was on his. Her tongue slipped in next to his and he froze. It felt like the world faded away.

"Get down!" James's forceful whisper slapped him harder than any punch could, "There's people out there."

"How many?" asked Sean, drawing his pistol.

"Only two. One of them is sleeping and the other dude is wearing fucking armor and is a giant!"

"Armor? Like tactical body—"

"No! Like fucking knight in shining armor... armor!"

Sean regarded James with an incredulous smile. Out in the middle of the woods, surrounded by wild packs of feral demon-children hell bent on eating them alive, and he gets worked up over someone's delusional King Arthur behavior.

"So he has a sword and shield, too?"

"No, he has some kind of metal ball on the end of a handle. I didn't see a shield or anything like—"

"It's called a mace," spoke a soft, gentle voice behind them.

The three kids spun around in unison. Sean raised his pistol while James shouldered his AR-15. Elizabeth fumbled with her .22 rifle. Even though James had done his best to prepare the group, the sight of the man in front of them was unsettling.

Standing at least six and a half foot, covered in a coat of several thousand metal rings, and looking at them through eyes red from crying was a young dark haired man wearing glasses. He held his arms out wide in front of him; empty hands outstretched.

"Take it easy. I'm not going to hurt anyone."

"How the fuck did you get behind us?" James stammered in awe.

The tall man took stock of the group in front of him. His eyes finally settled on the dog tags James wore. A smile spread across his face. "Z.O.D. member AOE-858 reporting for duty, Sergeant."

Sean and Elizabeth gaped up at the man while James slowly lowered his weapon. "You're Z.O.D.?"

"I joined right before shit hit the fan. I mean like an hour before the fallout rain started to come down."

"So there was radioactive rain?" Elizabeth gasped.

"Up in St. Louis there was. I was at a convention and the news started telling everyone to plastic up their windows and to seal their doors. It wasn't long after that those creatures—"

"Zombies," exclaimed all three kids at once.

"—Zombies burst in and started ripping people to shreds."

Sean and Elizabeth looked at each and then lowered their guns. James shook his head from side to side. "So how did you make it out of the city? Zombies, toxic rain, and I bet more than a few unfriendly people were against you."

"There were twenty of us. We had guns and grabbed vehicles where we could. The roads were so jammed only motorcycles could make it through at certain points. The Army had a lot of roads blocked and they actually fucking shot at us when we came close. It took a few hours to get out of the city. A few hours and… a few lost lives."

James slung his assault rifle over his shoulder and looked up at the tall man who seemed to be on the verge of tears again and frowned.

"So you and your friend are the only ones that made it

this far?"

"He's not my friend. I don't know him from Adam. He's just somebody that needed help. My name's Ethan."

"Well, let's get a litter made and get him back to camp. I'm sure Justin will have some questions for him... If he's sober enough to ask."

"It started when Weak13 had been invited to play some colleges here in the states. Neel and Wesley, my drummer and bass player, were just as excited as me about the tour. All of us were pumped."

"Starting in New York, we had gigs at Columbia University and NYU. From there it was a few cities that would lead up to our final performance at UCLA. Philadelphia, Pittsburg, and Cincinnati were all fantastic shows. The other bands in the tour were cool enough, but Weak13 was definitely the standout rock act."

Justin and Mark listened to Nick's story while Cindy, a middle-aged school nurse, tended to his cuts and bruises. James, Sean, and Elizabeth were busy skinning the game they had collected. Ethan was still wearing his armor. He sat in a folding chair absently munching on some dried meat James had given him.

"Everything was going great, man. Everyone was happy. We were making money from CD's and shirt sales. The sky was the limit and we were talkin' about extending our tour. Maybe find a manager here in the states and just keep rockin'. Then, the fucking apocalypse hit and we were stranded in bloody Rolla fucking Missouri!"

Nick took a drink from the canteen Mark offered him and sniffed his nose hard. The foreign plants were playing hell with his sinuses and it seemed more snot was forming with each passing breath.

"Me and my mates got separated when the beasties sprang up. Once I escaped the confines of the city I found myself stumbling through unfamiliar terrain. After a few days of scavenging for food I found a small house in the woods to squat in."

Nick looked over at Ethan and nodded his head toward him. The rocker ran a hand across the bald half of his scalp unconsciously flipping stray strands of dyed red hair back to the left side of his head.

"The little buggers found me this morning. I killed one of them, then Sir Ethan saved my ass from the others."

Ethan looked down at the ground and mumbled, "I wish I could've done more."

"No, mate! You did plenty saving my sorry ass. I owe you. I'll owe you 'til breath isn't in me anymore!"

Mark snorted. "So you've just been wanderin' aroun' the countryside since it all started?"

Nick stared at the older man. "Yeah, enjoyin' myself a fine fuckin' holiday at it!"

"Calm down. Both of you," Justin's gentle voice cut the tension. "Nick, I'm glad we found you. Ethan, it sure does sound like you saved the day. Both of you are welcome to stay here."

"What—" Mark began before Justin stopped his question with a scowl.

"We will figure out how you can contribute tomorrow. We have guards posted, so for the rest of today try to rest and get some of your energy back."

Ethan continued to stare at the ground while nodding.

"These are all superficial," Cindy cut in. "You will be fine in a day or two."

"Thank you for your help. Sincerely, I mean it. All of you. I'll pull my weight for as long as I'm here."

"You already have plans for leaving?" Justin asked as he handed him a freshly roasted rabbit.

Nick took a few quick bites. "Aye, my lady's back at home. I need ta' find a way across the bloody Atlantic. I don't suppose any of you Yanks can fly a plane?"

The question hung in the air for a moment before Nick laughed. "It never hurts to ask, eh?"

Small chuckles greeted the rocker from everyone except Mark. The older man stared at him and shook his head. He stood up and shouldered his rifle. Without a word he walked away from the group and into the woods.

"What's up with your friend?" the Brit asked between bites of his delicious meal.

"His wife and sons were killed when the children woke up." Justin intoned mechanically.

Nick slowed his chewing down. His thoughts drifted to home. Not knowing if his family was alive, dead, or turned into monsters had been in the corner of his mind since everything started. He couldn't imagine the children on his lane suddenly tearing at the flesh of others without a shudder. He knew it was the world over dealing with this shit. He could only hope that his home country was dealing better than America was.

The hope was dim as he looked around at all the armed people in the camp. There were more guns within ten meters of him than he had seen in his entire life. He couldn't wrap his brain around someone easily killing these demons with knives and clubs. The rocker felt tears coming to his eyes until he looked over at Ethan. The young man was now leaning back and sleeping peacefully in a chair much too small for him. If the lanky giant could take five of the bastards out, then he was sure an Englishmen might just stand a bit of a chance after all.

"For every animal of the forest is mine, and the cattle on a thousand hills. I know every bird in the mountains, and the insects in the fields are mine."

Psalm 50:10 -11

ALL THE PRETTY LITTLE HORSES

The beam was a huge chunk of oak that weighed a good hundred pounds and covered most of the existing door. Matt was discouraged when he first saw that it was the only thing that they had to barricade the opening with. His injured ankle made it difficult to carry any extra weight and he didn't want to rely on someone else to take his guard shifts. He was thankful that John found a solution to their dilemma.

Matt let the rope slip from his hand when he felt the beam shift against the door. Using the rope and pulley to lift the heavy door block in place had been one of John's ideas. John had a lot of ideas. Some were good, some were so-so, and some like the rope and pulley had been pure genius.

Rich, a large barrel chested man, was sweating from the exertions of fortifying the small country house. He had been welding and boarding up windows and doorways for the better part of two hours. Even though he was heavily muscled, his stamina was not the best. Digging into his shirt pocket he produced one of the reasons why.

Rich lit the cigarette and inhaled deeply. He coughed a bit as he expelled the smoke from his lungs. A worried look from Matt drew a chuckle from the big man and he offered the former Marine a hand rolled one. Matt waved it away. The two men sat down next to their AK-47s and popped open water bottles. Each took long drinks as they examined their handiwork.

The windows had been covered in steel with only a few slits left open as viewpoints, another idea of John's. Rich, welding and bending, finally managed to get them done and he was proud of the job. He didn't think it would take as long as it had. He was just happy it was finally over.

"Do you think John has any fancy ideas on how to make it through the winter?"

Matt pondered the question. They had been lucky enough to be the first ones to get to Bem Church and grab the food that was stored there. They had plenty of canned goods and grains. The house they found had an old fashioned water pump and it's well produced enough fresh water for everyone. Heating, however, was an issue. The house was all electric and had only a very small, thin metal chimney. A wood burning furnace was going to need to be found or constructed if they didn't want to freeze to death. A new exhaust system would need to be implemented along with it.

"I'm sure 'Big Brain' will figure out something," muttered Matt between sips of water. "He certainly has earned his nickname a hundred times over."

Placing the cap back on his water bottle Rich nodded in agreement. The portly man had been an engineer at some factory in Jefferson City. Rich and Matt had found him while they were out scouting for food and convinced him that he had a much higher chance of survival with a group.

"That's the truth!" chuckled Rich while exhaling smoke, "Man, all we need now is a doctor or a few hot nurses and we are set!"

"That would be nice. Hell, I'd settle for a fully stocked drug store. Doctors are mainly pimps for the pill companies anyway. Why not just cut out the middleman?"

"I'll give ya' that one. But, you're not going to talk me out of wanting nurses!"

Matt, snorting with laughter, cuffed the big man on his

shoulder. "Fair enough. You keep the nurses and I'll keep the drugs."

"Deal! How's your ankle holding up?"

"It's getting better. I think it's just a sprain. Still hurts like hell when I put a lot of weight on it."

Both men fell into an uncomfortable silence. Jacob had been a good man and a joker. He had always been willing to help out and a hard worker. Matt owed his life to him. When the group had been jumped by a pack of creepers it had been Jacob who pulled one of the beasts off of him. Even though they managed to kill them all, somehow the little bastard had infected the poor man.

Jacob had joked about the thing 'snowballing' him after the incident. His jokes turned into worry for his friends after an hour when he complained about the taste of struck matches in his mouth. That evening he was violently ill, throwing up and feverish, but he seemed better by morning. He was even back to making jokes… and laughing.

Over the next week Jacob's laughing fits grew worse until they were forced to gag him and tie him up. While they were talking about his fate he went completely still. Kevin, a former classmate of Matt's, went to check on him and all kinds of shit went down.

Jacob burst through the bonds that held him, and he snapped Kevin's neck like it was a dry chicken bone. He was laughing and smiling as he attacked others with his bare hands. Rhonda was his second victim; he ripped her throat out with his teeth. His blood soaked smile was almost comical as he slaughtered two others in rapid succession, Blake and Robert, by slamming their skulls together as they tried to flee.

Lauren almost made it out of his reach, but slipped in the blood coated grass and went down. The madman leapt on her. Matt charged in to tackle him, but at the last possible second Jacob somehow managed to throw him off balance with a brutal swipe from his arm. He spun away from his failed rescue attempt, twisting his ankle painfully. Jacob, still cackling madly, was pounding the hapless woman's head into mush when Father Murray was finally able to put a bullet in his brain.

"It wasn't anyone's fault, dude." The big man set his water bottle down and made eye contact with his injured companion. Matt looked away and stared at the oak beam barricading the door.

"I know. I've just… Rich, there's so many people I've lost. So many I couldn't save." Matt had talked about the incidents faced by he and Thomas as they escaped Owensville. Rich had known Matt's friend Justin, always liked and gotten along with him, and he knew that Matt felt responsible for the drunk and the kids he left in the tool shed.

He understood how the former Marine felt. Rich had lost people too. The big man couldn't find any words of comfort for himself let alone someone else. Matt had been on edge about the incident since it happened. He expressed his desire to go look for them several times, but the hard fact of the matter was he had no idea where to even begin the search.

"Done for the day?"

The unexpected voice startled both men. Glancing up they saw Father Murray staring down at them smiling. "It looks like you two really busted your butts. The windows look good Rich! Matt, that beam rig is really making it easy for you to move that heavy lump of wood, eh?"

Standing quickly with the aid of the wall behind him Matt faced the priest. "Yeah, it's pretty easy now."

The former Marine stared at the smiling man. Rich could feel the tension between the two pressing down on him like an invisible weight. One on one both of them were pleasant to be around, but when they were together it was unsettling. Neither of them was rude to the other, but their conversations held an undertone of palpable loathing.

"Good. I'd hate for you to get hurt again. It's hard to say how much more you can take."

"Don't worry about me, Father. I'm sure that I'll be as right as rain in no time. Hell, I might even be able to run soon. You're a runner… right, Father?"

Rich thought he saw Thomas's eyes narrow for a moment, but from his vantage point on the ground it was hard to tell.

"It's good exercise and keeps you healthy. It's a shame so many people never pick it up." Rich chimed in trying to defuse the volatile feeling conversation.

"You're right. The conditioning of one's body really makes a difference these days." Father Murray nodded toward Rich while speaking, the smile never leaving his face.

Matt's brow furrowed and he clenched his teeth. He knew the priest was talking about his friend Justin. The smug bastard was still smiling at him. *One of these days I'm going to knock all your fucking teeth down your throat you twisted fuck.*

"Enough about exercising, I just wanted to let you two know that the grill is full and lunch will be up in no time. John just tapped that keg of home brew he made and it is shaping up to be a good day."

Rich stood up and stretched his sore muscles. "That sounds great. We could all use a day off from this shit."

"I'll be out in a bit. I wanna' practice getting this thing on and off the door a few more times. I still get hung up with this damn pulley every now and then."

Shrugging, the big man grabbed his AK-47 and headed off toward the rear exit. "Okay, dude. I'll try to save you a beer or two."

The priest and former Marine watched as he walked out the door. Now alone both men regarded each other with cold stares. The false smile dropped from Thomas' face as he considered the injured man in front of him while Matt's hands shook with barely controlled rage.

"I saved our lives. The least you could do — "

"Bullshit you fucking coward!" Matt spat the words toward the corrupt priest, "You saved your own ass. I was just the unlucky fucker who happened to be with you. You left them to die! Justin, the kids… everyone!"

"What could I have done?"

"You should have went back for them!"

Thomas let out a snorting laugh. "And then what? Bury what wasn't eaten?"

"You son of a bitch!" Coming from his clenched jaw the words were barely coherent. Realizing he may have finally pushed the other man too far the priest took a step back.

Matt's head was pounding. He took a few deep breaths in an attempt to calm himself. Eventually he would kill Father

Thomas Murray. He knew he would, but now wasn't the time.

"There is a reckoning coming, Father. There are no laws anymore; nothing to keep you safe except for the person next to you. Once you show your true colors around here I may find myself standing in line to kill you."

The priest spun on his heels and strode toward the rear door. The injured man watched him fling the door open. He turned back to practice on sliding the beam into place when he heard the door slam behind Father Murray. Matt felt a little better knowing he struck a nerve with the bastard.

He worked with the beam another ten minutes. Even with the help of the pulley it was still a mild struggle for him to keep extra weight off his injured ankle. After securing the beam for the final time he slumped down next to the door and slowly moved his foot in a small circle. Grimacing in pain he stretched out on the thin carpet and stared at the pale white ceiling.

A loud crashing from outside jolted him to a sitting position. He cocked his head to the side and listened as the noise was suddenly amplified by dozens of screams from the people on the other side of the door.

Matt clamored to his feet and grabbed the rifle next to him just as gunfire erupted. He rounded the corner to the hall and was only a few steps from the rear door when it unexpectedly flung open. John came rushing through clutching his left shoulder. Blood spurted in huge gouts from a wound much too large to be covered with a hand.

The pudgy engineer made it a few steps toward him before collapsing. His face was pale from blood loss. His eyes were wide with shock. His mouth was opening and closing involuntarily while his legs shook violently; as if they were still trying to run.

Gunfire continued to sound from just outside the door and Matt could also hear shrieks from injured people accompanied by squeals of delight from demonic children.

BREEHT! A loud bleating noise like nothing he had ever heard before echoed along with the rest of the cacophony.

As he neared the door Rich came flying through the opening and smacked loudly against the wall. A quick glance at the prone man lying unmoving in a pool of John's blood confirmed his fears. Rich's head was caved in and was only held on to the body by a thin flap of skin. His neck bones and upper spinal cord were poking out of jagged rips in his flesh.

Matt quickly leaned down and checked John's wound. It looked like something huge had taken a bite out of him. John stared up at him and feebly tried to reach out to grab his arm. Matt placed his hand on top of the dying man's and gave a strong squeeze. Standing up he lowered the weapon's muzzle against his doomed friend's head and pulled the trigger. *CRACK!* The sound signaled the last of his friend's earthly pain.

Peering out of the doorway his jaw went slack. Matt had witnessed his share of strangeness over the last few months, but nothing had prepared his mind for the sight awaiting him. A pair of giraffes, along with several demonic children, was running rampant in the backyard.

The animal's fur clung to the beasts in ragged patches. The exposed greyish-green skin was oozing yellowish puss. Long, sickly tongues covered in white splotches swung limply from twisted and oversized blood coated jaws. Their spindly legs had jagged bone projections growing out at various angles and were being used to devastating effectiveness as the monsters bucked and lashed out at his friends. *BREEHT!* The beasts roared.

Many of the creepers were fighting each other over fresh corpses. Some were happily ripping chunks of meat away while others tried dragging bodies into the woods. Only a few of the twisted children were still engaging the survivors.

There was only five of his group still alive. Using a flipped over picnic table as makeshift cover they were hard pressed to fend off the creatures. Melissa, a cute short blonde-haired woman with an ample chest, was frantically shooting a .30-30 Winchester at the foreign animals. Adam, AK-47 firing, was trying to drop one of the giraffes along with her, while Billy and Erik swung baseball bats at anything that got close. Father Murray squeezed off round after round from his pistol striking the fast moving creepers in the head with deadly accuracy.

The guns spat a steady stream of burning lead into the giant animals. Chunks of corrupted flesh were ripped away as bullets tore into their soft hides. The enraged animals were healing as fast as they were being injured. They charged the small group.

The first beast to reach the barrier was greeted with a hail of gunfire and wildly swinging bats. Its momentum was violently halted by the barrage. The stench of sulfur permeated the entire area as most of its chest disappeared in a yellowish mist when the shells shredded the animal. Stumbling awkwardly to its right side, the wounds began closing on the stunned monster. The second giraffe galloped in fast on the heels of the first. Snapping its head down the creature clamped its jaw around Adam's right arm and AK-47. Twisting its head and yanking back the monster severed the appendage at the elbow and snapped the gun in two.

Adam stumbled backwards screaming and clutched helplessly at the wound. Blood was erupting in a steady stream covering everyone close to him. Billy was momentarily distracted by the sudden spray of gore. He didn't see the creeper jumping at him. Slamming into his chest, the force of the grey-mottled demon drove him to the ground and stole the air from his lungs. He was helpless to react as the small misshapen beast, once a three year old girl with bright blue eyes, sank her teeth into his cheek while tearing at his neck with wickedly sharp talons. His blood quickly joined Adam's on the ground.

Seeing his friend on the ground Erik swung his bat like a golf club at the monster on Billy's chest. A sickening *crunch* rewarded his strike as the hell-child was flung over the picnic table, screeching as it flew. Bending down to help his wounded friend Erick felt hot pressure in his lower back and suddenly lost all feeling in his legs, but he didn't fall.

The burning sensation in his back intensified as he was hoisted in the air. Erik stared dully as the bat slipped from his nerveless hand while three more creepers swarmed over Billy's body. He watched helplessly as his friend weakly tried to push the hungry children away. His vision was abruptly shifted and he was staring at a beautiful clear blue sky. He grew dizzy, but then felt peacefulness seep into him. His vision shook and he could feel his body jerking back and forth. The last thing Erik saw as he tumbled away from the giraffe's mouth was his lower body separating from him just before he hit the ground.

Matt crouched inside the doorway and brought the AK-47 to his shoulder. "Get in here!"

The former Marine sent several shots flying in rapid succession at the giraffe that had just ripped Erik apart. One of the bullets caught the creature in the upper jaw, snapping through bone and exiting the top of its skull. The gigantic beast toppled over pinning the three creepers busy feasting on Billy's twitching corpse underneath it.

The remaining giraffe was now fully healed. It lashed out at Father Murray with its front legs. The priest leapt back as the blows came crashing down where he had been a fraction of a second before. Melissa, hearing Matt's commanding shout, made a break for the open door.

Melissa's sudden move caught the attention of the rampaging beast and its dull, lifeless eyes were focusing on her as she ran. Matt fired two more shots then was shocked by a resounding *ching*.

"God damn it!" he cursed as he yanked the useless magazine out and slapped a full one in. Chambering a cartridge as fast as he could, he raised the weapon fearing he was already too late to save her.

Turning in pursuit as Melissa bolted for the door the giraffe's hellish eyes burned with rage. Greenish spittle rained down from its twisted maw as its long legs easily began closing the distance on her.

Before the world turned into a living nightmare she had been an avid jogger. She had run marathons and dashes for fun, never imagining that her hobby would one day be essential for survival. Her body was conditioned by all the training she had poured into it over the years. She was no stranger to the necessity for bursts of speed. She barreled past Matt as the monster swung its long neck down towards her.

Colliding with the house the giraffe was knocked on its haunches. *BREEHT!* The animal bellowed its anger at being denied its prey. Trying to get it away from the door Matt fired more rounds into the monstrous beast's belly. As the giraffe retreated he saw Thomas skirting the patio and making his way towards the house with a small pack of four creepers in tow.

Years of military maneuvers and combat experience allowed Matt to analyze the situation in an instant. The giraffe was out of its stupor and charging the doorway. Father Murray waved his hands frantically at Matt while running. His eyes were wide with terror. There was only a small chance he would win the race against the hell-spawned beast and the creepers were almost on him...

Without a second thought the former Marine slammed the door shut trapping the priest outside.

The fallen priest's eyes narrowed into dangerous slits when Matt closed the door. *You mother fucker!* He cursed in his head, *I'm going to fucking kill you!* His thoughts on revenge shifted to survival upon hearing the stomping hooves of the giraffe and the evil giggles of flesh eating children.

Thomas, seeing no alternative, spun around with his pistol raised. The creepers were less than three yards away. Aiming for the head of a gangly little boy who couldn't be older than five he squeezed off two shots. The first one struck the monster in its neck and the second one connecting in the center of its forehead. Bone and brain matter exploded out of the back of the child's head. The gore spraying the remaining demon-spawns as they rapidly closed the distance on the priest.

Seeing movement out of the corner of his eye Father Murray dove to the ground. The giraffe, running in to trample him, knocked the creepers violently away and began bucking. The twisted kids screeched having landed painfully several yards away. From his prone position under the animal the priest rolled frantically trying to avoid the flailing limbs.

First one, then another, then the last of the creepers launched themselves at the enraged animal. Biting into its putrid flesh with their razor sharp teeth and ripping away at rotten skin with their talons the demonic children lashed out in vengeance at the animal.

Thomas rolled as fast as he could. He cleared the dangerous ground underneath the giraffe as it jumped and kicked to dislodge its former allies. Seeing that the fiends were busy trying to tear each other apart the priest continued his run to the backdoor.

"Let me in! Let me in God damn it!" Father Murray pounded on the door. From inside he could hear someone fumbling with a lock.

"The keys broke in the door!" Melissa's voice echoed from behind the wood, sounding panicked. "Get to the front I'll have it open for you!"

Fuck! Sprinting to the corner of the house he lurched to a stop underneath a hanging oil lantern when the overpowering stench of death hit his nostrils. After looking around wildly for a moment his gaze finally fell on something moving through the woods.

He took a slow, deep breath as the creature lumbered into the clearing. The sounds of the giraffe and the creepers faded away as Thomas numbly stared at the decaying elephant casually walking towards the front of the house.

"A fucking what?"

"An elephant… it's an elephant!"

Matt still couldn't believe what Melissa was yelling. Watching the creepers and giraffe taking their fight further away from the door gave Matt the break he needed to check out the situation in front.

As he navigated his way to the screaming woman he saw Melissa peering out of one of the barred windows. Joining her all he could do was stare in disbelief. Standing in the front yard was an elephant.

Its once grey skin was now a dingy black and covered with huge white splotches. One of its ears was hanging close to its left front leg. It was holding on by only the barest scraps of skin and muscle. The lower half of the trunk was missing. A jagged tear the only sign it had ever been there. Yellowish mucus drained from the severed appendage and from its left eye socket where the orb was dangling freely. The tusks of the creature had grown vicious, serrated barbs. Pieces of bloody clothing hung from the gruesome bone colored ivory.

"It's a... Fucking elephant!"

"I told you!"

Watching the creature walk unhurried toward the house sent waves of panic screaming through Melissa. She had seen live ones at the St. Louis Zoo every time she went there. They had always seemed so playful and carefree... A stark contrast to the monstrosity that was heading straight for the house.

"Can that thing break down the door?" Melissa said quietly, trying to keep the fear from her voice.

"That thing can tear down this entire place!"

As if understanding what Matt had said the beast suddenly lunged forward with phenomenal speed towards the house. The former Marine grabbed Melissa and pulled her as fast as he could toward the rear of the building. After being dragged a few steps, she turned and ran for all she was worth.

As they were rounding the corner to the hall leading towards the rear door the entire house shook. Loud cracking from destroyed timber exploded from behind them as the outer wall gave way to the force of the elephant's impact.

Tripping from the shifting foundation Matt plunked down heavily on his side. Melissa wasted no time. She tightened her grip on his arm and yanked him to his feet. Running, the pair of them neared the back door. Matt stopped for less than a heartbeat to shoot the lock. Kicking with all the strength he could summon he flung open the damaged door.

Melissa was right behind him as he barreled out of the collapsing house. She saw that both of the giraffes were down and unmoving and no creepers were in her field of vision. Behind the pair the house continued to rumble as the powerful beast continued its charge.

This gun won't make it through that things skull! We won't be able to outrun it... we're fucked! Matt was on the verge of screaming in desperation. *It's eye! Small as hell... but it's our only chance!*

"Keep running!" Not waiting to see if she obeyed his order or not, Matt spun around and brought the AK-47 up to his shoulder. He struggled to control his breathing as the rotting pachyderm erupted from the debris.

He fired shot after shot. Each one striking the animal in the face, but missing the eye sockets. He didn't even know if the rounds were penetrating the skull or not. He did know with certainty that the animal kept getting closer with each passing second.

Hearing a loud CRACK from behind him made him grit his teeth. It seemed Melissa had ceased her escape and was firing on the beast. He wanted to rip his hair out in frustration. *She should have kept running!*

Matt and Melissa were so focused on the elephant that neither of them saw Father Murray throwing the freshly lit lantern. The old glass crushed when it connected to the monster's body and the oil exploded in a fiery ball. Flames licking at the hide of the beast easily ignited the dry skin. Roaring in pain, it ran through the woods setting small fires where chunks of its burning body fell away.

Matt and Melissa were still shaking from adrenaline. They clung to each other. Without thinking Melissa kissed him. Matt although surprised eagerly returned the affection. Knowing that at any instant they could be dead only heightened the sensations they were feeling at the moment. Each of them wanting to experience everything life could offer before it was taken from them.

"Keep on making out," the fallen priest panted. "I'll grab what food and water I can."

Matt and Melissa broke their embrace. Each one looking a little embarrassed about what had just happened. With the effects of the adrenaline wearing off Matt could feel the pain in his ankle screaming for attention.

"I'll give you a hand," Melissa offered seeing the former Marine's face scrunch up in pain. "Matt get off your foot while you can."

Matt nodded as he slowly allowed himself to crumple to the ground. *That thing was a rotting mess! Why didn't it heal like the others?* He could still see the burning elephant running through the woods. On any other day he might have laughed about it. He watched as the animal fell over and burned. He watched until the tears falling from his eyes blurred everything out.

"For the moth will eat them like a garment, And the grub will eat them like wool But My righteousness will be forever, and My salvation to all generations."

Isaiah 51:8

4

BUTTERFLY, BUTTERFLY, LAND ON ME

Resting from the mornings work, Nick and Ethan leaned against the posts on the front porch of Clyde and Emma's old house. A gentle breeze blew through camp causing small pockets of dirt to form into miniature tornados.

Nick watched the dust devils spinning among the buildings and walls with a smile on his face. Ethan chuckled at the sight of the hard core rocker being so fascinated by a little wind and dust.

"What are you laughing at, man?"

"Well, this bad ass leather wearing rocker from the UK is pretty amusing."

"Fuck off ya' scrawny wanker!" Laughed Nick.

In the week that followed his rescue at the hands of the kid they had grown close. Both of them were outsiders trying to fit into a small community of people they had almost nothing in common with.

Ethan still wore his chainmail armor. The dark-haired

young man now carried a shotgun to compliment the mace he had strapped to his hip. Nick wore his freshly patched leather jacket and gloves. He had been grateful that Darlene was a saddler and knew how to work with leather. With a little convincing he had talked her into putting some metal plates on the knuckles of his gloves. It seemed that no matter what else was around he would always end up punching the little fucks eventually.

Sitting in a rocking chair above them and humming softly, Firmin was busy polishing a magnifying glass he had found. The Frenchman could remember using such a device to start fires when he was a kid and he was looking forward to trying it out again. He couldn't understand any of what was being said between the new folks, but it was good to hear laughter.

"What are you humming up there, Monsieur Firmin?" Ethan asked, trying to include the foreigner in the conversation.

Hearing his name he looked down at the young giant and waved the magnifying glass. "Pour faire un feu. Ou brûler les fourmis si vous aimez ce genre de chose," he happily chirped then resumed his humming.

"Pretty language. Too bad we can't understand you, mate."

"It was something about fire. 'Feu' means fire… I think."

"Feu. Feu," Firmin nodded excitedly toward Ethan.

"Well… So long as he's happy about it," Nick yawned as he stretched out his shoulders. "How long will those strips of meat last ya' think?"

Ethan pondered the question. He had no experience with food preservation outside of using a refrigerator. He did find the process of drying out the meat interesting, but he hadn't asked Mark too many questions while he helped him with the task.

He still felt out of place. He knew the odd looks thrown his way were more about the armor he wore than anything to do with him personally, but he still felt uneasy under their gaze. Out of everyone in the camp, all twenty-two of them, he was only comfortable with six.

Nick and Firmin, outcasts like him, got along great. Justin was nice, though he seemed to like drinking more than making idle conversation. Sean and Elizabeth were a cute couple and they had gone out of their way to make him comfortable. James was a trip. The kid took everything serious and was fanatic about 'zombie' defense. Still, he seemed very genuine in his actions.

"Earth to Ethan! You in there?"

Nick's voice snapped him from his thoughts. "Sorry, my brain took a detour."

"I could see that, man. You was staring at your shoes like they grew wings." Nick chortled suddenly, "Oh that would be a lark! Sir Ethan flying about like the Greek god Hermes himself!"

Nick playfully slapped Ethan's knee as he continued laughing. "Or maybe... Who's that other chap? You know... The war guy!"

"Ares."

"Yeah, mate! That's it! Ares! You in your armor flying around, now that would be a sight!"

Ethan's laughter joined the rockers. Echoing through the camp it drew stares from everyone. Seeing the attention he was getting the young man did his best to stifle the commotion. Nick, noticing the glares of disapproval, laughed even harder.

After a few moments the Brit's laughter faded. He took out a handkerchief and blew his snot infested nose as hard as he could into it. "Don't these blokes know we're all going to die? They need to lighten up a bit. Look on the bright side of life while they can."

The armor clad young man smiled at the rocker and softly started whistling a tune from *The Life of Brian*. Picking up on the familiar melody Nick joined in. Both men abruptly turned towards Firmin when he added his whistling to theirs.

The three grinning men, whistling away, watched dust devils dancing on the dirt road until the breeze carried them away.

Mark's face was red as he stomped from the camp. Clenching his jaw and forcing himself to calm down he began taking more measured steps. He could still hear the idiots whistling behind him. *Don't they fucking understand how exposed we are?*

Weaving between trees and underbrush with scarcely a sound, the old survivalist put the group a good mile behind him. Squatting down next to a crabapple tree he dropped his pants.

Quickly relieving himself the old man wiped with toilet paper he brought from the camp. He took a few moments to cover his feces with loose soil and foliage before continuing on his way.

His destination was Rosebud. Even though the town had been turned into a burnt out wreck after the monsters came he wanted to do a thorough search of the general store to see how much fuel remained in its underground tanks. Clyde had been smart enough to store hundreds of gallons for emergency use, but it wouldn't last forever and he wanted to have a plan when it ran out.

The woodsman's dread had been growing continually after witnessing the strange black cloud flowing from the dead man's mouth on Highway 19. No matter how hard he tried convincing the other people at camp they needed to get the hell away from all kinds of civilization no one listened.

They thought they were safe. He knew they weren't. He knew that at any time a horde of the demon-spawned children could overrun their walls and rip them to pieces. Or that one or two of the big brutish beasts could stumble upon them and cause even more damage. *Damn fools! How can they ignore all this shit?*

Mark had more than once considered taking all the food and ammunition he could carry and head off on his own. The only thing that stopped him was the admiration he had held for Clyde. Even though his friend and his friend's family had disappeared he knew he couldn't disrespect his memory like that. Sighing deeply, Mark resigned himself to stay with the group as long as he could.

Continuing through the woods he made it to town just as twilight was settling in. With civilization all but wiped away there were no streetlights, headlights, or houselights to interfere with the beauty of the natural world. A half-moon lit up the night accompanied by a host of stars. The celestial light brought the landscape alive in ways Mark hadn't seen since he was a boy on his grandmother's farm in Michigan.

Feeling nostalgia beginning to creep up on him he allowed himself a rare smile before forcing the unwanted emotion away. His life had been simple before the big snooze put all the kids down. Enjoying retirement, his wife and him had been living in the house they bought in the country. Their sons were grown and out of the nest. He could hunt, fish, or just tinker around in his workshop anytime he wanted to.

Thinking of his lost family brought a lump to his throat. He had killed seven of the little bastards, but not before they had taken everything he loved from him. He had placed his family's bodies on the couch near each other and set the place the on fire.

With a pistol in his mouth he was ready to join them in whatever afterlife was willing to accept his soul. In those last moments his mind drifted to thoughts of the people he knew that might still be alive. People that might need him. Before realizing what he was doing he had already walked halfway to Clyde's.

Kneeling down and using a fallen tree for cover he forced the memories away as he concentrated on the scenery before him. Even now, months after the big snooze, the smell of smoke and soot clung to the remains of the town. Ash blown by the wind created deep drifts against buildings and covered the streets. All that remained of once beautiful homes were collapsing brick walls dotting Highway 50.

Hugging the outskirts of the city limits the old man moved quietly along toward the lone standing metal sign that once marked the location of the general store. Looking closely Mark could make out individual houses from the piles of rubble. Listening, all he could hear was debris getting displaced by the wind. Making sure the noise wasn't any of the little creepers he cautiously moved from wreckage to wreckage towards the general store.

Mark slinked along the ground the last forty feet to the cap leading to the underground tank. Shifting through ash he was surprised to find the cap already off. He tied a bolt to the end of bailing twine he carried and lowered it into the tank. He grimaced when a metallic *clank* echoed up from the empty tank.

Well, at least that means other folks are still alive... or at least were. The sobering thought that they were going to have to compete for the limited resources remaining slammed into him. *Every man for himself.*

Imaging his group going up against another one in a fight made him shake his head in frustration. Hoping he could convince them to head deeper into the woods Mark slowly worked his way out of town and back to the camp.

"I don't know what to tell ya', Mark. Most people just don't want to leave."

Scowling, Mark listened as Darlene explained the consensus of the group to him. He had gotten in late last night and expressed his concerns of their safety to Justin, Darlene, Cindy, and Joe. Squabbling ensued that nearly led to a fight between the old survivalist and Joe. The younger man had laughed off the idea of leaving as paranoia. Justin barely managed to keep fists from flying, but in the end his calming presence won out. It was finally decided that they would ask the members of the small community what their opinions were in the morning and then have a meeting at noon to discuss options. So far it was not going well.

"So the ones that want to stay won't let the ones who want to leave take any supplies? That's bullshit! We have just as much claim on the food and water as anyone!" Mark slammed his hand down on the table with enough force to tip over the candle holder in the center.

"Let me ask you sumtin'... How exactly do you plan on stopping us?"

Darlene and Cindy looked at each other in shock while Joe leaned back in a wooden chair with his arms crossed. A smug smile spread over the younger man's face at how worked up Mark had gotten. Justin slouched against the front door whether in defeat or from a hangover was anyone's guess.

"We'd beat your asses!" Joe laughed, "There are a lot more people staying than going, you old bastard."

Mark's lips trembled as his face suddenly flushed an ugly reddish hue. With a sudden clarity of what was about to happen Justin opened the door and stood to the side just as the old man leapt over the table at Joe.

"You som' bitch!" Slamming into the younger man Mark's momentum carried them both out the door and onto the porch. He clasped Joe's neck firmly in his left hand as his right landed punch after punch.

Sitting at a small picnic table across the dirt road Ethan and Nick watched dumfounded as the combatants rolled onto the yard screaming incoherently at each other. Leaping to their feet in unison both men lunged forward to separate the two men.

The old man's punches felt like a hammer pounding on his face. Feeling his nose crunch with the first strike Joe knew he was in serious trouble. The subsequent blows on his face wracked him with hot pain. Joe was desperately trying to grapple Mark's hand from his airway so he could breathe. The lack of oxygen was weakening him and his vision grew blurry. Right on the verge of blacking out the pressure on his throat suddenly disappeared and he gulped in a large lungful of air.

He tried standing, but his legs didn't have the strength. Collapsing face down on the lawn Joe felt a heavy throbbing in his head. He heard raised voices above him but, between gasping for more air and the pounding in his ears he couldn't understand what was being said.

Rolling on his back he finally understood the cause of his sudden freedom. The strange Brit was holding Mark in a full nelson and was whispering something in his ear. Ethan stood in front of Mark and was rubbing his shoulder. Justin, Cindy, and Darlene stood on the porch looking down on the aftermath of the brief struggle.

Stumbling, Joe rose unsteadily to his feet. Feeling warm liquid flowing down his chin he gingerly touched his nose. Pain erupted through him as he confirmed it was broken. A metallic taste pooled in his mouth and dripped down the back of his throat. He spat the blood on the ground along with two of his top front teeth.

"I'll fhuckin' 'keel eew'!" Joe slurred while fumbling for the knife at his belt.

Seeing the movement Nick let go of Mark's arms. "Don't do it, man!"

Catching the warning tone in his friend's voice Ethan spun around as the bloody man finally managed to free his knife from its sheath. Without thinking the tall man took two steps and threw a right cross. His fist connected squarely with the belligerent man's jaw. The blow dropped him where he stood.

The confrontation had drawn the attention of the whole camp. Hushed whispering accompanied the crowd that was fast gathering around the scene. Backing up the stairs, Ethan and Nick eyed the more boisterous of the mob members. Kneeling calmly next to Joe, Mark took the knife from the unconscious man's clutched hand and slowly walked up the stairs to stand next to Justin.

"What the hell happened?" Derrick, a thin middle-aged man and friend of Joe's, demanded.

"Cocksucker threatened me!" Mark motioned his head toward the still unmoving man. "You don't do that shit with me unless yer' ready to back it up!"

"Is this about you wanting to take all our food and leave?" Someone called out.

"Wait, now hold on!" Justin stepped forward. "No one is taking all the food. No one is taking all of anything. Mark and a few other folks don't want to stay here so—"

"Fuck him then! He can get his ass out of here." Kneeling down next to Joe, Derrick looked up as he continued, "But he ain't gonna' take any of our food with him. Neither is anyone else who leaves!"

Justin's face wrinkled in frustration as he listened to the rant. He knew that short of killing him there was no way anyone could stop Mark from filling his backpack. *He deserves it, too! Much more than most of these damn people do!*

"There's plenty enough to go around, ya' fucking tosser!" Nick exploded.

"You haven't been here long enough to get anything!" Another man in the crowd yelled out, "You're lucky we even let you stay!"

Rolling his eyes Nick glanced over at Ethan. The lanky giant had his arms crossed low on his stomach, His right hand lightly touching the handle of his mace. Understanding the danger they were in if it came to blows Nick shook his head slowly at Ethan. *Better off alive and hungry than dead and full.*

Mutterings from the crowd ranged from whispers to all out insults hurled towards Mark and anyone else who wanted to leave. Knowing the situation was quickly escalating out of hand Justin whispered to Mark, "Do you have a plan to get us out of this?"

"I thought you was stayin' put?"

"So did I! Now..." Justin shrugged hopelessly. The vehemence of the crowd gave him a sudden flash of insight. Looking out among them all he could see was self-centered and greedy people willing to step on others to get what they want. There was no way this community would survive the winter.

"Okay, everyone calm down!" Cindy's normally sweet voice sounded angry, "I know things are tense and we're all scared. We still don't know what really happened or how this is all gonna' end, but we can't fight each other! That'll just tear us apart!"

Growing quiet for a moment the crowd looked at each other. A few people were talking in harsh tones and continued to glare at those on the porch. Most of the ruthless glares were focused on Mark. Clenching his jaw tightly he returned them; daring anyone to challenge him again with his eyes.

"No one is taking anything from this camp!" Derrick called out.

The outburst sparked more yelling and threats from the mob. Justin looked down at people he once felt close to. Now they were fingering weapons and looking like they were ready to kill him at a moment's notice.

Not understanding anything that was being said Firmin stood off to the side of the mob. Having watched the incident since it spilled outside he knew that the old man had beaten the younger one pretty badly. Witnessing the knife being drawn he was worried about an escalation in the violence. All around him the Americans were shifting on their feet or fiddling with their guns. It wasn't a good sign for a peaceful resolution.

He wasn't a coward by any means. He had been in his fair share of scuffles and was a former savate instructor. His ability with a firearm was virtually nonexistent, however. He had never had the opportunity to train with one and the 9 mm tucked into his belt was more for show than anything else. If it came down to shooting, he feared he would do more harm than good for his friends Ethan and Nick.

Realizing no one was paying attention to him Firmin shuffled to the edge of the cabin and then flattened himself out along the side wall. If things were going to get out of hand he wanted to make sure he was out of the line of fire.

More shouting echoed from around the corner of the building. The Frenchman's mind raced for a solution to the situation. Balling his hands into fists he beat them in frustration on his legs. Communicating with the Americans beyond the simplest of words was impossible, and judging by the rising clamor it would be useless to even try.

The Frenchman slid along the outer wall and slipped around the corner. Behind the cabin now, he pulled out his pistol. Running as fast as he could Firmin made his way to the wood line. Passing the first large tree he stopped and turned. He couldn't see anyone following him, but he heard more yells. Forcing himself to slow his breathing he kneeled next to the trunk of the tree.

Movement to his right caused his head to turn. At first he thought it was a low hanging cloud until it got closer. Butterflies, hundreds maybe thousands, were gliding silently toward the camp. Getting closer, Firmin could make out crimson wings turning into a dull orange at the tips. Their bodies were a more subdued red and black.

Firmin was an entomologist in the old world. He had always found butterflies delightful to work with. He enjoyed their colorations and the way they moved, almost like dancers. His momentary distraction turned into recognition when one of them landed near him on the tree.

It was a Madrilenial Butterfly. His excitement at seeing the species quickly turned into confusion. It was only native to Spain. *What are you doing here, little friend?* He moved in for a closer look.

Its proboscis was unusually long and appeared to have a barbed hook at the end. The legs, in turn, ended in the same hook-like appearance. Leaning in closer he was dumbfounded to find that they weren't legs at all, but additional proboscis. Feeling a chill wash over him the Frenchman stood cautiously still. A small gasp escaped him when he remembered that the Madrilenial Butterfly was most famous for feasting on blood.

Freezing as the insect took flight, Firmin held his breath as the abomination fluttered in circles a few times before landing on the back of a rabbit he hadn't noticed a few yards away. The rabbit, its eyes on him, didn't seem to notice it had a passenger.

Unable to look away he watched as the butterfly viciously impaled the animal with all seven of its hungry mouths. The rabbit hopped straight up in the air then fell on its side, legs still kicking. It spun in three fast circles and then convulsed. The animal's breathing was fast and strained as the butterfly continued to drain some of its blood.

The swarm of malicious insects was almost to the cabin. The yelling continued to get louder from the camp. The Frenchman knew he had to warn them. Sprinting from the woods as fast as he could he rounded the corner of the cabin. He slid to a stop when he saw guns being pointed between the two groups.

"Chercher! Ces papillons sont mauvais!" He waved wildly in the direction of the swarm. "Courez pour vos vies!"

His sudden outburst snapped the tension long enough for a few heads to turn. Soon everyone was looking at the approaching mass of bugs. Firmin bounded up the stairs and grasped Ethan by the arm, pulling him off the porch. "Nous devons aller ... MAINTENANT!"

Ethan let the Frenchman lead him down the steps. Nick and Justin followed behind while Cindy and Darlene stood open mouthed at the sight of the approaching insects. Mark, using the butterflies as a distraction, crawled over the side of the cabin and began working his way to the food stores in the next building.

Opening the door he was surprised to find James, Sean, and Elizabeth busy stuffing food into backpacks. The old survivalist scrunched up his face. "What the hell ya' think you're doing?"

Continuing with their work Sean responded for them. "We heard what was happening so while everyone was acting like assholes we grabbed food for you."

"For us, kid. I'm taking all of you with me. It isn't safe here."

"But—" Elizabeth began.

"There's no time to argue. I think Justin is coming too, along with that lanky kid and the English guy with half a head of hair."

Snatching the full backpack from James, Mark headed back out the door. Squinting his eyes against the sun he saw Firmin running with Ethan, Justin, and Nick. Screams suddenly erupted from the crowd as people began dropping and rolling along the ground when the butterflies landed on their exposed flesh.

Derrick couldn't get Joe to wake up and he was worried. *That damn kid really put you out, man!* All around him were wings and a humming *buzz.* The butterflies were landing on people.

While everyone else was giggling about the bugs he was gently shaking his friend. He offhandedly brushed away a few that landed on Joe's face. One stuck to the back of his left hand so he squashed it. A slight smell of burnt matchsticks hit his nostrils.

More of the insects landed on him and his friend. He swatted each with enough force to spray their juices across several inches of his skin. Each time he killed one the odor of sulfur grew. He started to pull Joe away from the mass of insects, but stumbled back when he saw three of the creatures attach themselves to his face. Their legs throbbed as blood was drawn from the helpless man. More of the insects landed on his friend and joined in the feast. Derrick leapt to his feet.

"IT BURNS!" Cindy grabbed him as her scream quickly replaced the laughter she had let loose when they first landed on her. Derrick shoved her away.

"GET THEM OFF ME!" Screeched another voice behind him.

Derrick felt liquid fire erupt from the back of his neck. Before he could react he was on his back. Rolling as best he could to dislodge them his mouth and nose quickly filled with the stench of burnt matches. Derrick tried to stand. Fiery agony spilled down his legs as more of the hellish insects began feeding on him.

Collapsing on the ground shaking, he watched helplessly as Mark and a small group of others fled into the forest. His limbs, numbed beyond the point of feeling, twitched and shuddered. He couldn't even scream when one of the butterflies landed on his right eye and shoved one of its proboscises into his pupil.

"But as for the cowardly, the faithless, the detestable, as for murderers, the sexually immoral, sorcerers, idolaters, and all liars, their portion will be in the lake that burns with fire and sulfur, which is the second death."

Revelation 21:8

5

I'M SQUISHING UP MY BABY BUMBLE BEE

Gagging, Melissa clamped her hand over her mouth as she left the house. The stench of rotting flesh and sulfur covered the exterior of the home and permeated the property. His mouth curling up in disgust at the odor, Father Murray quickened his pace after her toward the driveway where Matt was waiting.

Strewn about the yard were the twisted forms of small children. Initially deformed by whatever had taken control of their bodies, they were now completely unrecognizable from various stages of decay and having their heads caved in.

Stumbling across the house had been lucky, even though all they found were empty cupboards inside. The real treasure was discovering two four-wheelers locked in the small detached garage.

Melissa and Thomas had waded through the corpses to search the house for keys while the former Marine stood guard outside. Fortune had smiled on them when they entered the kitchen and found them sitting on the table along with a handwritten note:

If you need the 4wheelers these ar the keys. Take um. My boys are buried out back. All I ask is you thank them for tellin me to buy them. There names are Jacob and Josh. They were good boys. Theyre in heavan now.

Reading the note several times had left Melissa's face streaked with tears. She hadn't seen her own son, Dylan, since he had left in February for San Francisco State University. He had gotten a baseball scholarship, and they needed him there for spring training. The last time they had talked was right after people had been stricken with the comas. She didn't know if he was safe or—

"I think you should ride with me." The priest's voice broke her train of thought.

Looking back at Thomas she felt uneasy at the way he was staring at her. His eyes seemed too intent and focused on her tits. His smile was almost predatory. Shivering from a sudden chill racing down her spine she crossed her arms over her chest. "Matt still isn't in top shape. I'm going to ride with him in case he needs help."

Father Murray's smile twitched as she turned away from him. Watching her perfectly toned ass swaying as she walked, the fallen priest fantasized about how it would look wiggling on his face. Allowing the scene to play out in his mind, he felt a surge of jealousy when she climbed behind Matt onto the yellow four-wheeler and whispered in his ear.

"We're going to find the kid's graves in the back," Matt called out. "The least we can do is pay our respects."

"I'm right behind you." *Waste of fucking time!*

Thomas sat on his ATV and turned the engine over. Starting off slowly he tried to get a feeling for the steering and balance. It had been a long time since he had ridden one, and he didn't want it flipping over on top of him.

Maneuvering to the rear of the house he found Matt and Melissa kneeling next to two mounds of dirt and rocks. Matt was holding the woman close to him and Thomas could hear her crying. *That stupid bitch is losing her shit! She doesn't even know who she's crying for!*

"Fa... Fath... Father, could... could you say a prayer for... for them?" She asked between sobs.

The fallen priest could barely suppress his laughter. Quickly covering his outburst with fake coughing he composed himself. "Of course, my child, of course."

Father Murray made the sign of the cross and bowed his head. "O merciful God, Whose property is always to have mercy and to spare, we humbly beseech Thee for the soul of Thy servants, which Thou hast commanded to depart out of this world. We ask Thou wouldst not deliver it into the hands of the enemy, nor forget it unto the end, but wouldst command it to be received by Your holy angels, and conducted to paradise, its true home; that as in Thee it hath hoped and believed, it may not suffer the pains of hell, but may take possession of eternal joys. Through Christ our Lord. Amen."

As the prayer was coming to a close a cool breeze sprang up. Light at first, it quickly grew until tree branches were whipping in the wind. The leaves began shaking so violently they made a hissing sound.

Standing quickly Matt and Melissa shivered from the unexpected cold snap. The former Marine leaned on the shorter woman as they walked back to the four-wheeler, his ankle still recovering from the chaos of the previous day. She helped him get settled and grasped him tightly around the waist after she climbed on back.

The fallen priest stood next to the graves for a few moments fighting down a wave of dizziness and nausea that washed over him as he finished the prayer. The queasiness slowly faded away just as the wind began dying down. Thomas stumbled over to his ATV and slumped over the seat. Sweat poured from his face and soaked his shirt. Fast replacing the dizziness was a throbbing headache.

"Are you okay?" The question seemed to come from far away and Father Murray couldn't tell if it was Matt or Melissa who asked him.

"I'll be okay; just my breakfast disagreeing with me."

Leaning in so close he could feel her breath on his neck, Matt's grip tightened on the handle bars as Melissa whispered,

"He looks like he is going to pass out."

Glancing over his shoulder, the former Marine eyed Thomas critically. "Were you bit the other day?"

"No. I'm just… Not feeling well. It musta' been something in that stew we had."

Matt got off the four-wheeler and took a few steps towards the fallen priest. He was still leaning over the side of his seat and his eyes were closed. Moving closer to him he could see the man's legs were shaking. Reaching out, Matt yanked the pistol out of the priest's holster.

Father Murray bolted upright. He made an awkward grab for the weapon, but toppled over as Matt shuffled out of his reach. Fighting waves of sickness Thomas climbed onto his knees and held out his hand. "Give me back my gun!"

"Are you sure you didn't get bit?" The edge in Matt's voice sent a shiver through Melissa as she watched.

Biting his bottom lip Thomas shook his head and wiped sweat from his eyes. "Yes, I'm sure."

The former Marine leveled the pistol even with the kneeling man's head. "Melissa, turn around." Bringing his hands up in a futile defensive pose Father Murray's eyes widened with surprise.

"You can't shoot him! We don't know if he was bit or—"

"I'm not going to shoot him. Thomas, this is what's going to happen. You're going to slowly stand up and take off your clothes. If I see a bite, I'm putting you down. Understand?"

Father Murray's mouth curled into a snarl as he got to his feet. Pulling his shirt over his head he glared at Matt. Melissa turned around as the priest began removing the rest of his clothing.

Matt's expression didn't change as he watched the fallen priest. Father Murray was now wearing only his underwear and socks. He stopped stripping. "Is this good enough?"

"Yeah. That's fine. Turn around slowly."

Thomas held his hands in the air and spun in a slow circle. The sick feeling in his stomach was gone and his head felt much better. Sweat had ceased falling from his head and his legs had regained their stability.

"Okay. You're clear. I'm sure you understand why I had to

check. We wouldn't want another incident like the one we had with Jacob."

Father Murray pulled on his pants and forced a smile. "Of course. We have to make sure we're all safe, even from each other."

Matt and Thomas locked eyes. Both men knew that it was only a matter of time before one of them put a bullet in the other. Looking away, Thomas finished putting his clothes on.

After tucking in his shirt the priest held his hand out. "My gun."

Matt briefly entertained the notion of blowing the man's head off his shoulders. If Melissa wasn't standing just a few feet away he would have already done the deed. Instead, he reluctantly handed the weapon over.

Thomas slid the pistol into its holster as Matt walked back to his ATV. His hands, still shaking from the bout of illness that stole over him, clutched the handlebars as he climbed on the four-wheeler. He turned the engine on and felt the machine vibrating underneath him. Matt and Melissa were pulling slowly away from him and heading into the woods.

Matt had found a trail behind the house and was focusing on navigating the rough terrain. Melissa held on to him and rested her head against his shoulder. The fallen priest followed closely behind, his imagination still playing out images of how her naked body would look on top of him.

In his other life he knew her as Miss Roberts the teacher who had given him detention for talking too much in class. In that other life he spent the evening after his punishment egging her house with one of his friends.

Laughing at how much work it would take her to clean up the mess the boys had giggled themselves to sleep that night. True to their plan, the next morning at school the middle-aged brunette had dark circles under her eyes and was snippy to everyone. But, that was another life.

Now her blood stained dress was shredded to the point where it only hung in rags from cold, pallid skin. Her left leg ended in a stump. Her foot had been viciously ripped away by hungry, needle-like teeth. Her head tilted awkwardly to the left and jagged pieces of collarbone jutted from bruised skin.

Flies buzzed around the carcass as the boy pulled it along behind him. Stopping only occasionally to rip a piece of rotting meat from the woman's corpse and stuff it in its mouth, the deformed child-beast continued its march through the woods.

It was nearing the destination as the sun began to set. The sweet smell of decaying flesh greeted its nostrils. Cackling in delight the child hastened its march. Drawing closer to an abandoned house the creature was soon joined by others. Each of the twisted children carried or dragged the corpse of a person with them.

The once bright white siding of the house was now stained deep brown in several spots; remnants of where blood from past feedings had splashed. Mold grew along the gutters and down the sides of the windows; tendrils of rot and deterioration spider-webbed its way across the front porch. Decaying bodies were piled in front of the house as a macabre offering to the lone occupant. Laughing grey-mottled skinned children scampered around eagerly waiting for an appearance from the dweller.

Creeping towards the house the deformed child plopped its prize down next to a red-headed man with his jawbone and skull exposed. Bite marks covered his face and neck where the skin had been peeled away. After placing the mangled body on the pile it quickly retreated while giggling, leaving an opening for the next beast to take its place.

A shuffling emanated from inside the house as the last of the twenty-seven creepers arrived. Each of the creatures froze at the sound. As one, they followed the noise with their eyes as it grew closer to the front door.

Stopping just on the other side of the entrance, the dweller waited while those outside began wailing. The clamor grew until the windows were shaking. Still, the dweller waited. The frenzy of the creepers boiled over and they began leaping back and forth. Still, the dweller waited.

Losing patience, a small female creeper missing its right arm leapt onto the porch. Immediately the four largest beasts wrenched it back to the ground. Hissing, they tore into the smaller one ripping and tearing while it screeched in pain.

The door flung open. The enforcers instantly released the offender and shielded their eyes from the soft reddish glow that flowed from the house and bathed the front yard in its light. Following suit, the rest of the monsters did the same. Whining softly, the injured one stayed crumpled in a ball not daring to move.

Stepping out of the door in long purposeful strides was a young woman. A reddish glow emanated from her eyes, blanketing her face in soft light. Small framed, she barely topped the five foot mark. She wiped her hands on the front of her light denim overall shorts, leaving streaks of blood in the fabric. Taking a moment she plucked a firefly from her tanned leg and squished it before focusing on the scene before her.

Hopping off the porch she landed next to the wounded creeper. She knelt down while brushing soft blonde hair away from her pretty face. Her deep blue eyes narrowed and full lips parted in a grimace while taking in the damage of the creature. The wounds were slowly healing. Glancing up, her gaze washed over the four responsible. The red glow emanating from her eyes intensified.

"You know little Alice wasn't trying to get in front of anybody. She just wanted to see me!" Her voice was low and piercing. The four enforcers fell on their faces and groveled in the gore soaked dirt. She ignored them as she gently enfolded Alice in her arms.

"She doesn't heal as fast as most of you," still holding the wounded creeper the dweller rose to her feet as she spoke, "Things are different now! I know you all want to grow, but you're my children! Never forget that! I want you small forever".

The glow from her eyes gradually dimmed until only a faint aura of red encompassed her face. The creepers sidled closer and Alice wrapped her arm around the dweller's neck. The woman looked into the warped eyes of the creature she held and smiled.

"Now, let's see what you've been up to."

The lady pulled Alice's face close to hers. The creature

became perfectly still and wide-eyed. The dweller put her tongue on the left pupil of the monster she embraced. Whirling from a sudden barrage of images, her mind and the creatures became one for just an instant. She watched as the demon opened its eyes for the first time in the child's body. She watched as tears of joy turned into screams of confusion and horror as little Alice ripped her mother's throat open with razor sharp teeth. The dweller smiled when Alice's father slipped in his wife's blood and struck his head on a pew, knocking him unconscious.

Watching such carnage unfold at a church sent waves of delight through her. She relished in each scream, in each cry for mercy, and especially at each unanswered prayer for salvation. Feeling it start as a soft tingling in her stomach, she was soon aroused and could feel her wetness soaking through the skimpy thong underwear she wore. So intent on enjoying the visions and the feeling, she was caught completely off guard when Alice wiggled out of her arms.

"Hey! I wasn't finished!" She moaned.

The little creeper hopped around the yard giggling. Panting softly, the dweller motioned for another one of the beasts to approach her. One after another they came to her. Each one sharing images of their memory with her in the same way as Alice had done. She would kneel and place her tongue on one of their pupils. Memories played out with each child-beast offering a different perspective on the slaughter. The brutality of those images, the blood and violence, drove her deeper into a lust-crazed frenzy.

After more orgasms than she could count, only one creature remained to be read. Soaking with sweat and pleasure, she beckoned it to her. Licking its pupil she was drawn into the past again. This one's actions were particularly heinous. She whimpered in raw ecstasy as the child bashed in his mother's head and lapped up the leaking gore before cracking her skull open wider to scoop out handfuls of brain.

She was on the verge of another climax when a painfully blinding white light exploded in her head. Collapsing on the ground she held her head and violently started shaking. The creepers stopped giggling and stood in mute shock. The dweller's body convulsed and gyrated. After a few minutes she shrieked.

The force of the unholy blare sent creepers reeling. All but one dug their claws into the ground to keep their footing. The lone, hapless creature that wasn't fast enough to brace itself was flung through the air and struck a tree headfirst. The magnitude of the impact pulverized its skull in an instant and sent the twisted child's lifeless limbs flailing.

Climbing unsteadily to her feet, the dweller quickly found the last creature she had been reading. Cowering next to the bodies near the porch it hid its head underneath long, gangly arms. She wobbled towards the whining demon-child, stumbling the last few feet and landing painfully on her side close to it. Hissing and yelping at their companion other creepers began closing in, intent on making it suffer for hurting the dweller.

Regaining her senses she raised her hand. "STOP!"

Subsiding quickly, only faint hissing echoed through the trees. Crawling forward the offending creeper rolled onto its back like a dog. Laying her hand gently on its head she forced herself to smile when the twisted child looked up at her.

Before the agony assailed her, she had seen a boy running through the church. He had been outlined in a faint golden light the likes of which she had never seen. Even thinking about it caused an ache to creep into the corners of her head.

Placing her other hand on its temple she forced her thoughts to clear. Moments later deeper memories from the hell-child came to her. She absorbed them. She examined each one that the other boy was in. She explored the feelings the occupied husk once held for him. She saw laughter and friendship shared between the two. She watched it all right up until the great darkness overcame the host's body.

Pulling away she sat quietly, pondering what course of action she should take. She knew there were others like her, different since the Rapture claimed the souls of the faithful and innocent. She had been told much by the mysterious voice that whispered in her ear nightly, but it never mentioned a boy's soul that was purposely left in its body. They didn't need anything like that in this new world.

The dweller casually reached out and tore a chunk of flesh from one of the corpses close to her. As she bit into the rancid meat squeals of delight erupted all around her as child-like monsters began tearing into the other bodies, joining in the feast.

Her free hand was still resting lightly on the creeper's head. She absently patted it while she chewed her meal. A low whining from below caused her to finally look down. The creature in her lap was staring at the hunk of flesh she was clutching.

Bringing the morsel to its deformed lips she smiled when it began feeding from her hand. She continued petting and offering it bites in-between her own mouthfuls. She laughed softly at the way the demon purred and giggled as she fed it. With a strength that was impossible for one of her size she ripped an arm off another corpse. The rotting meat easily fell away from the bone into her mouth. She hungrily chewed and swallowed several bites before offering the rest to the creature she held.

Feeling full and completely refreshed she stood and stretched. Fetid blood covered her face and trickled down her arms. She let the beast lick her hands clean, its rough tongue tickling her fingertips lightly. She gave it one final pat and stared deep into its inhuman eyes.

"Lewis," she purred as her eyes flashed brightly, "I think we will be seeing your best friend very soon."

The screams were fading behind them as the group ran. Firmin ran out in front of the group. He navigated westward purely by instinct. Nick and Ethan ran side by side with the kids close on their heels. Mark stayed behind the children to keep an eye on them and Justin brought up the rear.

"What the fuck were those things?" James panted as he ran.

"Bloodsucking butterflies!" Elizabeth gasped out.

It took every ounce of willpower he had to keep putting one foot in front of the other. Blindly running forward, his vision narrowing to almost a slit, Justin's sweat soaked through his clothing. The former pastor's chest and legs were burning from exertion. He had always intended to get into physical shape when this disaster struck. He had lost weight, but his drinking had gotten in the way of any kind of conditioning.

His side cramped painfully and his breathing was labored. He lumbered along, barely avoiding trees and fighting for every step through the harsh underbrush. Looking up, he saw the group pulling away from him. The adrenaline had worn off and his energy was fast failing him.

"Justin's done in." Mark called out. His voice was steady with no hint of fatigue.

"Firmin!" Ethan slowed his pace when the Frenchman turned around.

Nick, breathing heavy, leaned against the trunk of a nearby tree. James and Sean watched behind them as they readied their weapons. Elizabeth sat down and tried slowing her breathing. Justin collapsed in a heap at the edge of the group.

"Ke... keep going," Justin gasped. "I'll catch up."

Mark knelt next to the younger man and looked him over. He chewed his lower lip as he watched Justin panting on the ground with his eyes closed. The old survivalist slowly inhaled as he leaned in closer. "If you can't keep up we'll have to leave ya'. I'm not risking everybody's life. I know you don't want that either."

Keeping his eyes closed Justin nodded from the ground. He understood that distance was the best defense they could muster against a swarm of devil-touched insects. Justin had no illusions on what part he played in the 'you don't have to outrun the bear' scenario.

"Keep them safe."

Patting Justin on the shoulder a few times Mark finally stood and motioned for Nick and Ethan to join him a short distance from the group. "He ain't gonna' be able to run much farther."

"So we rest here?" Ethan stared at the old man.

Mark returned the gaze and didn't say anything. Nick looked over his shoulder at Justin sprawled out on the forest's floor and let out a deep sigh. With realization creeping in Ethan started backing away.

"No. No."

"Ethan, mate, we can't fight a whole flock of those fuckin' things. All of—"

"NO! HELL no! We don't leave anyone behind. Nobody else dies, Nick. Don't you get it? NOBODY else dies!"

Sean and Elizabeth looked at the grownups when Ethan was in the middle of his outburst. James grimaced as the conversation got loud. Placing his hands on a low hanging branch the Z.O.D kid scampered a dozen feet up the tree for a better vantage point.

"Quiet!" Justin muttered, struggling to sit up. "He's right. I'm slowing you all down."

"But—"

"No. Listen to him. Mark knows the woods. He'll keep you safe. I'll follow as best I can. Hopefully those damn things are flying the other direction."

"No such luck!" James yelled from his perch as he hastily began descending the tree. "They're heading this way."

"I'll stay with him." Ethan quipped, gritting his teeth firmly together.

"The hell you will, mate!" Nick knew Ethan would be inflexible in his stance. He wasn't going to let him throw his life away needlessly. The rocker yanked his glove off and balled his right hand tightly into a fist. Before he could change his mind he punched Ethan as hard as he could on the kid's chin.

Staggering back Ethan fell over a small log hidden under some leaves. He sprang up quickly, clutching his jaw. "The FUCK?"

Nick's mouth hung open for a second. The Brit smiled sheepishly and shrugged. "It was supposed to knock you out. It always works in the films so I thought I'd give it a go."

"Enough!" Justin climbed to his feet, still panting.

He glared at everyone at around him. "When, not IF, but WHEN I fall behind keep running. If I live, I'll find you!"

With that he started a slow jog. Firmin, nodding impatiently, matched his speed. Soon everyone was loping along. Ethan stayed next to Justin as they maneuvered through the terrain. James, Sean, and Elizabeth stayed in a tight group with the older boy stopping occasionally to look behind them for danger. Mark and Nick took up the rear this time.

The run lasted five minutes before Justin started slowing down. Ethan held his left arm and tried to help him, but the out of shape man finally stopped altogether. The kids huddled close to Justin. Mark and Nick stopped, knowing that they would have to drag Ethan away kicking and screaming. Firmin stayed in front of the group pacing back and forth.

"Ethan—"

"I know what you're going to say. I don't care. You're not going to be left alone."

Justin looked helplessly at Mark and Nick. "This is stupid. What good will it do?"

"Nobody else dies."

Justin slapped Ethan hard across the face. "You die! I die! Everyone fucking dies, kid! Heart attack, stroke, or killer fucking butterflies, it doesn't matter! We all die!"

Ethan clutched his face and took a step back. Firmin slowly walked toward the group while scanning the sky for the approaching swarm. James, Sean, and Elizabeth stared wide-eyed in shock at Justin's violent display. Nick put his hand on Ethan's shoulder while Mark nodded slowly at the former pastor.

Tears falling from his eyes, Ethan pulled away from Nick's gentle hand. "Why?"

"Because it's always been that way, mate. No better way to explain it than that."

Justin caught a glimpse of the butterfly swarm weaving in and out of trees. It was less than half a mile away. "Get out of here! Mark, get them all out of here!"

Sean finally understood. Justin wasn't able to run anymore and they wanted to leave him. The red-haired kid flushed as blood rushed to his head. *No way!* Before anyone could react he nudged his way past Ethan and Mark. Flinging his arms around Justin's leg, he sat down.

"Get him off me!"

Mark and Nick grabbed at Sean. Wiggling around as best he could to slip out of their grasp, the kid managed to stay latched onto the former pastor. Firmin joined in and succeeded in getting a grip on Sean's wrist. The Frenchman, twisting and putting pressure on Sean's forearm, broke his grip on Justin. As his hand came free Nick grabbed it and helped Firmin pull him away.

"Let me GO!" Sean flailed and struck out at the foreigners as they hauled him off Justin. He felt a burning sensation in his right hip. Looking down, he saw a wet spot spreading across his pants.

A putrid stench assailed the group. Nick, relinquishing his hold on the kid, covered his mouth and nose. Gagging, he stumbled back and bounced hard off a tree. Justin sneezed violently and pulled his shirt up to cover his lower face. Ethan's eyes watered and his vision blurred from his tears.

Remembering the reeking contents of the glass vial left James and Elizabeth a little more prepared than the rest. The two teenagers still coughed and gagged, but weren't completely overpowered by the odor.

Instantly recognizing the smell Firmin froze in place. He had no idea where Sean had gotten a hold of the stuff or even if the child knew what uses it had. Looking around he saw everyone's negative reaction to the scent... A smell that just might save them all.

"Se rapprocher de lui!" The Frenchman yelled grabbing Justin in his left hand and Nick in his right. He pulled them closer to him and the stinking boy. Standing defiantly Sean eyed the adults with balled fists.

"Firmin!" Justin shouted. "You all have to run!"

"Hold on a tick, mate!" Nick gagged out, "Seems Frenchy has a thought."

Letting go of Nick and Justin, Firmin pointed at James and Elizabeth with one hand while waving at them to come closer with his other. His movements were slow and exaggerated. A smile spread across his face when he looked at a confused Ethan stumbling toward him.

Everyone crowded around Sean. Mark and Justin nervously watched for the approaching swarm. Still smiling, Firmin began softly humming a song from his childhood. The unfamiliar tune sounded happy and carefree; a stark contrast to the terror that was flowing through everyone's body.

The old man chewed on his lower lip and slowly rocked back and forth on his heels. When the swarm came into view he felt his legs start shaking as adrenaline pumped through his veins. Every instinct Mark had screamed at him to get away from the crazy French bastard.

Looking over at Firmin who was still smiling and humming away he silently cursed himself for staying with the small group. As the demonic insects closed in he entertained a fleeting thought of making a break for it. Realizing that there was no way he could outdistance the bugs at this point he gritted his teeth and waited for them to attack.

The butterflies closed in on silent wings. Fluttering above the group, they paused. After a few heartbeats the swarm slowly began floating away. Slack-jawed, Mark and Nick could only stare as the killer cloud of insects disappeared deeper into the woods.

All eyes turned to Firmin. The Frenchman's smile was a comforting sight. "Le garçon avait l'huile de Neem dans sa poche. Papillons détestent huile de Neem."

Justin looked at the smiling man with awe. "Firmin, I don't know what just happened, or what you're sayin', but thank you!"

Pointing toward Sean, the foreigner's smile grew wider. "L'huile de Neem. Papillons et autochenilles détestent huile de Neem."

"For the word of God is living and active, sharper than any two-edged sword, piercing to the division of soul and of spirit, of joints and of marrow, and discerning the thoughts and intentions of the heart."

Hebrews 4:12

I LOVE TO GO A-WANDERING

They sat in near total darkness around a small, smokeless campfire Mark had built. Justin stretched out on the ground, his legs aching from the unaccustomed exertions of the day. Ethan and Nick were cleaning their guns while the younger kids were boiling water over the fire for soup. Firmin sat with his back to a large oak tree and whittled at a small, twisted branch he had found during their escape.

Mark, chewing his lower lip, couldn't hold his question back any longer. "Well, what's the plan? Where do we head off to?"

"Why do we need a destination?"

Sean's question caught Mark off-guard. "Because winter's on its way and we just lost the only place we had prepped for it!"

"If we can make it to the Mississippi River we can grab a boat and just head down to the Gulf." Ethan mumbled, "It should be warm enough there and plenty of fish to eat."

Justin sat up. "I think that's a great idea."

Nick nodded his agreement. "My mind was keen on using a water route."

Mark slowly took a deep breath. "Show of hands, how many people thought about using the river to travel south?"

All of the adults, along with James, raised their hands. Mark nodded. "That's why we WON'T follow the river. Every swingin' dick within hundreds of miles of the Mississippi will be on that water. That means a lot of people and a lot of trouble."

Ethan hung his head. "I hadn't thought of that."

"Don't worry, kid. I'm sure there are a lot of bodies floating down that river that didn't think about it either. Survival 101: Avoid the main routes."

"So what's your fuckin' suggestion, mate?" Nick piped in defending Ethan.

Silence fell across the camp for several heartbeats broken only by the crackling of the fire as each person rolled ideas over in their heads.

Mark finally spoke. "West. We head west. I think California is a nice idea. Yeah, they'll be a lot of people heading that way, but most folks have no clue how to avoid the worst of the mountains. If we head just a tad south we should be fine."

Elizabeth smiled at Sean. "I always wanted to go to Hollywood."

The redhead returned the smile. It was good to see her getting back to her normal self. After the concussion she had seemed distant somehow. Like part of her wasn't there anymore. Lately she had been worrying him. A few nights ago she began flailing and shaking in her sleep. This left her tired the next day and, when asked, couldn't recall any bad dreams.

"Ha! So, I'll be able to see tinsel town after fuckin' all? Maybe this apocalypse isn't so bad." The rocker snickered.

"That's a long walk." Justin groaned.

Ethan and Mark couldn't hide their smiles. Mark knew that after a week or two the former pastor's body would be more use to the exercise. All this walking was going to do him some good.

James snorted out a harsh laugh. "Do you honestly think we'll make it? Seriously?"

The small camp fell into an uneasy silence. Mark and James stared at each other while the rest of the group looked around. Ethan leaned his shotgun next to a tree and poked their small fire with a stick.

The young Z.O.D. kid finally had enough of all of his friend's delusions. He pointed an accusatory finger at Mark. "Everyone we knew was just killed by butterflies. BUTTERFLIES! The most harmless creature on this fucking planet! You think we're actually gonna' waltz our way to California?"

Taking a step forward Mark shoved James to the ground. Gasps echoed from behind the pair as the defiant kid glared up at him. Mark's face was red and his mouth twisted into a snarl. "No, I don't. I think if we wanna' live we have to have a plan. We have to have a goal to work toward. This isn't gonna' be easy. Our chances are slim. We have to fight monsters, the land, the weather, even other people. I'm not gonna' die without a fight. I'm not gonna' give God, or Satan, the satisfaction of seein' me dying easy!"

Wincing in pain, Justin slowly stood. The former pastor's feet were throbbing and he knew they must be covered in blisters. He stepped between the old man and young kid. Looking at the group he could feel defeat hanging in the air.

Sean and Elizabeth clung to each other, babes literally lost in the woods. Ethan continued to stare at the fire and Nick calmly wiped his gun barrel with a cloth while watching as events unfolded. Firmin seemed to be ignoring everything except for the wood he was working on.

Justin took a deep breath. "I know we're all scared. I know there's a long road ahead of us, no matter what we do. We have to stick together. To be honest I don't care where we go. I don't care what the plan is. All I care about is each of you."

Ethan looked up at him and smiled. "Are we going to sing 'Kumbaya' now?"

Nick snorted. "Sure, why the fuck not? We can follow it up with a drum circle."

"I mean it. I care about each of you. I love every single one of you."

Mark's face sagged a bit. The old man held his hand out to James. Taking the offered help, the young kid pulled himself to his feet. Both of them looked ashamed as they faced each other.

"Look, kid—"

"Don't worry about it. We're all on edge."

Justin grabbed both of them. Pulling his shocked companions to him he engulfed them in a hug. Ethan stood and wrapped the group closer together his long arms easily stretching across them all.

Firmin stood and placed his hands on Sean and Elizabeth's shoulders. He smiled and softly hummed the most peaceful little song the children had ever heard. The Frenchman pressed something into the boy's hand. Sean looked at it. Firmin had given him a beautiful carving of a butterfly.

Looking up in confusion, Sean caught the foreigner's gaze. The older man smiled down at him. "Il ya encore la beauté dans le monde."

Nick stopped wiping down his weapon and shook his head. The Brit stood and cleared his throat. "I'll kick it off then. *Kumbaya, my Lord, kumbaya…*"

Slipping through underbrush and over fallen trees Mark and James scouted ahead of the group. Mark was impressed at how stealthy the kid was. Given a few more weeks of practice and he would give any Marine sniper a run for his money.

James pointed at himself and then to a spot up ahead and to the left. Mark nodded and watched as the boy scampered away from him. Continuing on his course the old survivalist weaved his way around trees and kept bearing to the west. After several minutes he spotted James peering around a tree ahead of him.

Moving cautiously to the boy's side he froze when he saw what had the kid's attention. Below them was a small ravine. From his vantage point up on the bluff he saw a group of seven creepers. The hell-kids were standing in a small clump of overturned and rotten trees gazing up into the sky. The mixed beasts ranged from what looked like a three-year-old girl to a ten-year-old boy. All of them were covered in shredded clothing and filth. The combination of grey skin and dirt indeed made them look like walking corpses.

Sniffing the air the largest of the creatures spun on its heels and started tromping to the northwest. The rest of the twisted children followed suit. Almost as one the small pack crouched and slinked along the ground.

Mark and James watched as the monsters scampered through the uneven terrain. Using their wickedly sharp talons, they easily climbed the embankment. As they disappeared over the edge and out of sight the old man and kid breathed a sigh of relief.

Damn it. Now what? Mark wracked his brain. *That group will be a pain in the ass if we don't take 'em out!*

"Go back and get the others. I'll follow 'em to make sure they don't double back on us. I'll leave a trail you can follow."

"I can go after—"

Mark narrowed his eyes at the kid and roughly jerked his thumb over his shoulder. "No arguin'!"

Clenching his jaw James nodded and began to walk away. Mark grabbed his arm before he got out of reach. "Be fast and be careful!"

"Well this is just great!" Matt shook his head in frustration at the flat tire.

Melissa stood next to the now useless four-wheeler and shrugged. They were still alive. That was a win in her book. "At least we made it a few miles."

Matt did his best to muster a smile, but could only manage an amused grimace. The athletic woman put her hands on his shoulders and leaned against him. Unconsciously, Matt put a hand over hers and held it.

His thumbs bouncing impatiently on the hard rubber handlebars of his ATV, Father Murray looked down at the pair from his vantage point on the ridge. The fallen priest felt jealousy surging through him again as he watched the woman pressing her chest against the other man's back. *Fuckin' bitch!*

"Are you sure you don't need a hand?" The priest

hollered down.

"No, it's fucked!" Matt's voice was thick with anger, "We're coming up!"

Putting Matt's arm over her shoulder Melissa helped the wounded man up the small hill. The incline had a gentle slope to it, but with his ankle still sore every step sent small waves of pain through him. By the time the pair reached the top, the former Marine was drenched with sweat. Through his haze of pain he could see Father Murray glaring smugly at him.

Melissa retrieved her rifle from the side of the ATV and slung it over her shoulder. "It's a good thing we still have one. Matt can use it to stay off his foot."

Thomas did a good job of holding back a scathing retort. "Yes! It's very fortunate. He can even scout out the terrain ahead of us."

Melissa's blue eyes narrowed. She didn't want to be alone with Thomas. The logic in the man's idea was hard to argue with, though. Sensing her unease at the suggestion Matt kept an eye on her as he sat down on the four-wheeler. If she said anything about it he would refuse to go.

She finally smiled at Matt. "Yeah, that could really help out."

"Okay. So the big question is where do we go?"

Father Murray and Melissa shrugged. They had all been so focused on getting away from the hellish zoo animals that a final destination never crossed their minds.

Melissa's thoughts went to Dylan. "San Francisco."

The priest raised an eyebrow. "Why so far away?"

Seeing pain sweep across the woman's expression Matt nodded his head in agreement. "California is a good idea. It's going to get cold here quick and I don't want to freeze to death."

"So we go west? Like the pioneers?" Father Murray laughed, "We can't make it over the mountains this late in the year!"

Melissa's face fell. She knew her son was almost two-thousand miles away. She understood what a monumental task it would be in finding him. She held out hope that he fled the city when the sleepers woke up. Of course if he had where would he go? Feeling her world spinning out of control Melissa buried her face in her hands and burst into tears.

Matt shot the fallen priest an angry glare. Getting off the ATV he wrapped his arms around the crying woman he pulled her close to him. Matt gently rubbed her back as he felt tears soaking his shoulder.

After a few moments he gently pushed her to arm's length and pulled her hands from her eyes. "We can take a southern route. It's more miles, but less mountainous. If we can make twenty miles a day we should get there in about four months. It'll be hard, but doable."

Melissa threw her arms around Matt's neck. The former Marine held her close again and kissed her gently on top of her head. He didn't know why San Francisco was so important to her, but he silently swore he would get her there.

Father Murray's eyes closed to dangerous slits as he watched the emotional exchange between the two. Melissa pressed her body in tight next to Matt's; her tits jiggling as she stretched to get her arms around his neck. *You fucking whore! What's so special about that arrogant prick?*

Looking over her head, Matt eyed the priest's reaction. It seemed that the good Father Murray was finding it harder to hide his feelings. He silently hoped that Melissa would catch on and keep her guard up around him. If he could just have a few moments alone with her he could voice his concerns about Thomas…

Melissa let him go and stepped away. The brightness of her smile almost made the tearstains disappear. Matt felt peace slowly steal over him as he looked at her. For a brief moment it felt like there was hope left in the world. Then out of the corner of his eye he saw Father Murray drawing his gun.

Mark easily picked up the trail left behind by the creatures. He silently followed it along a westerly course keeping his rifle at the ready. The hell-beasts did nothing to hide their passing and soon the survivalist had a clear view of them.

The twisted-children lay on the ground roughly ninety feet

from him and were slowly inching their way up an incline in the terrain. He could hear muffled voices coming from the other side of the small hill.

The old man chewed on his lower lip. He could make out three distinct voices, but not what they were saying. That meant there was at least three people, maybe more, who had no idea how close death was lurking to them. He stretched silently on the ground next to a thorn bush and swiftly piled leaves and small fallen branches around his upper torso. When satisfied with his concealment he lifted his rifle and took aim at the largest of the monsters.

He kept the demon-spawn in his gun sight as the group of corrupted kids clawed their way to the crest. The voices had quieted and Mark fervently hoped that whoever was on the other side of the hill was paying close attention to their surroundings now. Letting his breathing slow Mark put his finger on the trigger and softly began to squeeze…

SNAP!

He froze at the sound of the branch breaking behind him. The creature closest to the top of the hill suddenly craned its neck toward the noise. The other beasts stopped moving and focused on the actions of the smaller child.

Cursing under his breath he realized it was some of his group when the clinking of metal combined with the disturbed rustling of leaves heralded Ethan's approach. The four deformed children closest to the bottom spun around and leapt silently atop low hanging branches.

Mark was momentarily stunned by the agility of the small monsters. He watched numbly as the three remaining creepers spread out and continued their ascent much more rapidly up the hill. Adjusting his aim from the largest he now had one of the kids balancing on a branch in his sights. He heard the sounds of his friends getting closer and hoped that his shot would be enough to warn both groups of the danger they were in.

The old man was just starting to pull the trigger when screams and a gunshot erupted from the other side of the hill.

Thomas couldn't stop himself. The sudden flash of hate and jealousy toward Matt boiled over into action. Without fully realizing what he was doing, Father Murray pulled his pistol out and raised it toward the former Marine.

He could feel his anger narrowing like the point of a knife. His fury was turning into a blade that could be used to cut away all of his frustrations in a single stroke. He saw fear in Matt's eyes. He drank the feeling in and relished the taste.

Matt grabbed Melissa and hurled her to his left. The woman started screaming before she even fell. As he lined up Matt's face with the gun he noticed what had caused her premature outburst. Three creepers were rushing over the edge of the hill behind Matt. Cold practicality slapped him in the face as he grudgingly shifted targets.

Understanding the murderous intent in the other man's eyes, Matt roughly shoved Melissa away from him. She screamed as she fell. Her gaze focused on something behind him. Hoping to keep Thomas's attention on him and give the woman enough time to defend herself Matt leapt to his right. To his surprise the priest ignored him and fired the gun at something else.

He glanced quickly at Melissa as she sat up and unslung her rifle. A shadow fell across his face causing him to instinctively roll hard to his left. Matt's maneuvering threw his body roughly against a creeper as the small beast lunged forward to attack.

Luckily, he had knocked the creature off-balance and somehow ended up on top of it. He clutched the beast's arms as tight as he could and pushed away from its torso. The move kept him just out of biting reach.

CRACK! CRACK! CRACK! Rifle shots echoed from the direction the monsters had come from. In answer, more shots rang out from Father Murray's pistol. Melissa was screaming and her voice was suddenly joined by a chorus of others a short distance away.

Another rifle shot fired much closer to him, then more

weapons were discharged from over the hill. The small creature underneath him hissed and growled with a savagery he never thought possible. Fetid breath from the monster churned Matt's stomach and he momentarily gagged. It only took the hell-child a split second to seize the moment and flip him over.

Through a haze of confusion the former Marine's blood ran cold when he caught a glimpse of Melissa lying motionless on her back. Father Murray was using the downed woman's .30-30 like a club to fend off attacks from a large creeper.

Now straddling him, the hungry beast slashed at his face with deformed claws. Matt gripped his attacker's arms as tight as his hands allowed and threw all of his weight into a roll. To his surprise the small fiend didn't struggle against the move. A moment later he was flung into the air when the demonic child broke his hold.

His back smacked the side of a small tree; painfully leaving him sprawled out on the ground with the breath knocked out of his lungs. A guttural wheezing erupted from him as the creature jumped back on his chest.

Giggling, the beast slowly leaned in with its mouth wide open. Sharp, needle-like teeth suddenly lunged forward at lightning speed only to snap closed less than an inch from his nose. Sucking in air through the pain Matt saw Melissa's delicate arms wrapped around the creeper's neck. She was pulling back on the beast doing her best to keep it from biting him.

Matt shifted his weight and pushed against the creature's chest. It flailed madly for a moment, one clawed hand ripping four deep gashes in his right forearm before it was yanked off his torso.

Melissa's smile froze on her face as three deformed creepers sprang over the crest of the hill. She tried to shout a warning, but all that escaped her was a scream of terror. Matt's reflexes were amazing. No sooner than she opened her mouth he was shoving her away from him.

Stumbling, she was unable to recover from the sudden movement and landed in a heap on the ground. The bark of Father Murray's pistol rang out behind her and seemed to echo loudly back at them from over the hill. She watched in awe as one of the creepers twisted oddly in the air. Somehow the priest had managed to blow the top of the beast's head off mid-leap.

One of the demon-children was on top of Matt. The beast struck out at the prone man again and again. Each time he narrowly avoided the attacks. The last of the monsters was rushing her. She could hear Father Murray's pistol firing a steady rhythm behind her. Melissa watched as bullets ripped through the yellowish hide of the approaching child. The burning lead gave her a few precious seconds and allowed her to regain her feet.

Sheer terror drove Melissa's actions. She yanked the rifle from off her shoulder and took aim. Jerking the trigger in haste caused her shot to go wide off its mark. Wailing in rage and pain from the priest's attack, the creeper bore down on her. Not having time to chamber a round, Melissa brought the rifle up across her chest to block a talonned swipe from the hell-child.

CRACK! CRACK! CRACK! Shots rang out from the other side of the hill, followed by screams. Continuing to keep the rifle in front of her Melissa ducked and weaved away from the beast. Retreating blindly, she tripped over a large branch in her path. Yelping in surprise, she instinctively let go of her rifle to break her fall as she toppled over. She watched dully as her weapon sailed through the air over her head.

Lying motionless on her back she stared vacantly up into the sky. The noise of gunfire and screams exploding around her seemed surreal. For a moment it felt like she was floating above her body and absently watching the scene around her play out like a movie.

Melissa's awareness of her predicament was rudely reawakened when the creeper she was fighting vaulted over her. Rolling onto her stomach she saw Father Murray swinging her rifle at the creature she had been fighting. She scampered back on all fours and jumped to her feet.

"Hoooofff!" Turning at the unnatural sound Melissa gaped at the sight of one of the twisted hell-kids on top of a still prone Matt. Without thinking she charged the beast and threw her arms around its neck. Pulling back with all her strength she managed to drag the flailing beast off of her friend.

Knowing the preternatural strength of her opponent, Melissa flung her legs around the demon-child's body and held on. Clawed hands lashed out at her blindly. She buried her face as low into the creature's back as she could. The stench from the twisted child began overpowering her adrenaline. The noxious aroma made her feel dizzy and, with the addition of the creatures thrashing movements, queasy.

Searing pain exploded on the top of her head as one of the child's talons raked across her scalp. Sucking in a deep breath between pursed lips, she gritted her teeth. Something warm and sticky ran into her eyes. She clamped them shut to fight the sudden burning sensation.

"Help me!" The hopeless wailing of her own voice frightened her almost as much as the monster she held.

The creeper looked over its shoulder for less than a heartbeat. That was all the time Mark needed to send a steel-core bullet through the monster's skull. The tiny head of the hell-child exploded in a spray of yellowish gore as the body fell twitching to the ground.

Two of the other creatures dove from their perches in the branches to land less than ten feet from his position. The remaining one bounded through the trees toward the sound of his approaching friends. Mark realized the enormity of his situation when the smaller of the two beasts flung a handful of dirt and other debris into his face, blinding him.

The old survivalist kept his wits about him. He let go of the now useless rifle and yanked his hunting knife from the sheath on his belt. He couldn't hear the creatures in front of him, gunfire and screams from all over the area were too loud to pick up any footsteps. Leaping to his feet he stabbed and slashed around him, hoping to keep them at bay until help arrived.

He kept his body moving not wanting to give them an easy approach. A stench hit his nose and he shuffled to his left still swinging the knife. He felt something heavy slam into his back. His legs went numb and he toppled to the ground. His chest hurt and he could barely draw breath. He smelled blood. Coldness began to creep in on him. He could feel his hands twitching, but had no control over their movements. Close to him he could hear children giggling.

Even weighed down by twenty pounds of metal, Ethan's long strides propelled him ahead of the group. Nick was close behind him and James had run off as soon as he had delivered the news of the creeper pack. He knew Justin, Sean, Elizabeth, and Firmin were intentionally hanging back so he didn't wait.

CRACK! A shot echoed from up ahead followed by a woman screaming.

CRACK! Another shot. More screaming.

Ethan brought his shotgun up to his shoulder and slowed his pace.

CRACK! CRACK! CRACK! He nearly fell over as Nick's AK-47 roared to life behind him. Patches of bark landed on him as bullets sprayed a small oak tree to his left.

Ethan's shotgun slumped to his side as he turned and gaped at the Brit. Nick's eyes were wide and his mouth was opening and closing slowly. The rocker stared at his weapon, then sheepishly met Ethan's gaze.

"I bumped the fuckin' trigger."

Before Ethan could respond a four foot tall gray-mottled creeper sprang between them.

The beast was wrapped in a tattered yellowish shirt and stained underwear with a small blue tractor embroidered in the material. As it landed, the hell-spawn lashed out at the tall man with one of its talons then spun to engage Nick. Luckily Ethan's armor absorbed the impact from the vicious swipe as both men fell back screaming.

Ethan brought the shotgun up to his waist and angled it at

the monster's legs. He felt the recoil from the gun as he pulled the trigger. In an instant the hell-child's lower right leg was severed by buckshot.

The creature's feral snarling turned into a pitiful wail as it toppled over. Quickly raising his assault rifle to his shoulder, Nick fired six rounds into the twisted kid. The body jerked from the impact of the bullets while screams still escaped from Ethan, Nick, and the beast. The last shot from Nick struck the base of its skull silencing the shrieks of the creature.

Breathing heavily and shaking, both men eyed the body on the ground. It continued to convulse while the stench of sulfur permeated the area. Ethan steadied himself against the tree that Nick had accidently marred with his rifle.

The younger man couldn't pull his gaze away from the tractor on the monster's underwear. Ethan dropped his shotgun and buried his face in his hands. Deep gasping sobs began rolling out of him. "It screamed like a child. Like a fuckin' seven year old child! Oh fuck. These are kids! Just kids! Why? Fucking why?"

The Brit kept his rifle firmly planted against his shoulder. James had said there were seven of them. *Where are the other six?* He scanned the area for more of the monsters. *Where the fuck is Mark? Where the fuck is James?*

Nick's heart went out to his friend, barely more than a kid himself. They didn't have time to waste on crying. The rocker grabbed the armored man's shoulder and spun him around. He yanked his friend's hands away from his face. "Ethan! Mark's out here alone somewhere and we got five fuckin' hell brats unaccounted for. Snap the fuck out of it! These aren't kids. These are ravenous, flesh-eating, fucking wankers!"

Tears continued to roll down the soft-hearted man's cheeks. He stared at Nick for a few seconds and nodded. He began to blink rapidly and shake his head before kneeling down and retrieving his shotgun.

Nick's blood ran cold at Ethan's expression as his friend stood again and faced him. No trace of any emotion was evident on his face. A blank stare was all that greeted the rocker when the taller man looked down at him.

"No one else dies."

Nick nodded his head, unable to speak past the sudden lump in his throat. Ethan spun on his heels and wracked another shell into his shotgun's chamber. The armored man sprinted for the crest of the hill. Nick followed closely behind. He fervently hoped Ethan could keep that promise. Not for Mark's sake or his, but for the kids own sanity.

A few bent twigs here and there along with an occasional footprint marked the trail the old man left for him to find. James followed the signs as fast as he could; fighting the urge to run so he could remain silent. The forest was quiet all around him; the only sound was wind fighting against leaves for passage through the branches.

He slowed his pace when he heard faint voices carried with the breeze. His legs shook as he readied his rifle, ready to spring in any direction as he continued moving forward. Eyes darting left to right in an almost cartoonish fashion, he scanned the terrain for any signs of Mark or other people.

A distant sound from behind froze him in place. It seemed oddly familiar yet foreign at the same time. He half-closed his eyes while his brain raced to make the connection. The dim noise gradually increased in volume. It started to sound like a hammer lightly tapping against nails. Metal striking metal. *That could only mean—*

CRACK! The sharp report of a pistol came from over a small hill to his right drawing his eyes there for just a moment.

CRACK! He flinched as a rifle roared from less than ten yards in front of him. He saw gun smoke wafting up from the ground.

CRACK! CRACK! CRACK! More shots echoed from behind him where he had just heard Ethan running through the woods.

James was awestruck as he watched two creepers land from the trees close to where the second shot had come from. He would have never seen them if he had still been following his friend's trail. Time seemed to slow down as he watched Mark rise from under a pile of leaves, knife in hand. The old man was twisting and turning as he slashed, with no apparent focus on the two creatures rushing him.

The Z.O.D. scout brought the rifle up to his shoulder and aimed at one of the beasts. He gently squeezed the trigger when he had a bead on the hell-child's head… it was at that moment Mark stepped in front of his sights.

James watched helplessly as Mark stiffened. The boy tried to scream, but his throat locked up. The only sound that came out was a soft gurgle. Mark slumped heavily to the ground in front of the creepers. James tried to raise his weapon, but none of his muscles were obeying his commands.

He couldn't even turn away as the two monsters leaned in close to his friend. He wanted to shut his eyes; wanted to block out the gruesome meal Mark was about to become. James could do nothing. His mind refused to process what he had just done.

The larger creeper bent in and sniffed Mark. It stood and looked around. Its gaze finally focused on James. The smaller one also rose and stared at him. As if on cue, both of the demon- spawns laughed. Giggling like the children they once were, they turned and bolted over the hill.

James dropped his gun and surged forward. Tears filling his eyes as he swiftly covered the distance between Mark and him. He collapsed on his knees next to his blankly staring friend. James ripped a bandage from his belt pouch and futilely pressed it into the gaping wound that was exposing Mark's lower right ribcage.

Sobbing uncontrollably, James straddled his friend and pumped hard on his chest. Each jostling move caused blood to flow freely from the old man's mouth and nose. James was oblivious to all the gunfire around him. He rolled off of Mark's corpse and lay on the ground panting. He looked over and stared into his dead friend's glazed eyes. His stomach twitched and he felt like he was going to throw up. He climbed to his hands and knees and dry heaved. His brain finally digested the importance of the continued gunfire. James stumbled as he got to his feet.

"I'm sorry. I'm so sorry. I'm so fucking sorry!"

The boy grabbed the old survivalist's rifle and ran on

unsteady legs to the crest of the hill where the last explosions of gunfire were fading away. Mark's vacant eyes silently watched him go.

Ignoring the deep gashes in his arm Matt lunged at the hell-spawn Melissa was wrestling with. The small woman was still behind the beast, but its thrashings were wearing her down. Matt knew it was only a matter of time before it broke free.

CRACK! Another shot came from somewhere close to the pair's right. He grabbed the creature's flailing legs and crossed them. "Get clear!"

Melissa unwrapped her legs from the creeper's torso and threw her weight forward. At the same time she let go and pushed against the demon-child's back. She scampered away as the move launched the monster off her.

Matt yanked at the creeper's legs and twisted; spinning the creature up to waist level.

He continued turning in a circle and stepped toward the tree he had been flung against. A sickening *thwack* greeted his ears as the monster's legs were jarred from his hands. The reek of sulfur brought a smile to his face. The smile grew wider when he saw the creeper's head had been caved in by the collision with the tree.

Where's the other one? The sudden thought made Matt spin on his heel. Melissa was leaning against the ATV gasping for breath. There was no sign of Thomas anywhere. He stumbled over to Melissa. "Where's the priest?"

"I don't know. I was knocked down and he was fighting one. He had my... You're hurt!" Melissa's eyes widened when she saw the blood flowing from Matt's arm. She threw open the bag on the four-wheeler and pulled out gauze and alcohol.

Matt sucked in a deep breath as she doused his arm with the fiery liquid. He continued to scan the area for Father Murray and the last creeper while Melissa covered his bleeding arm with gauze. He took a moment to stare into her dark, brown eyes and felt himself calming down.

His face was grim when he figured out their next move.

"We need to find Thomas so we can—"

"Step away from the ATV!"

Melissa and Matt gaped at the source of the command. A young boy wearing camouflage was peering from behind a tree at them, an assault rifle aimed in their direction. A tall man wearing something that looked like a chain-link fence held a shotgun on them. A man in a leather jacket with long red hair growing only from one side of his head had an AK-47 trained on them.

The former Marine and jogger looked at each other and then back at the trio that had them at gunpoint. Matt tensed his muscles ready to buy Melissa time to get away, even at the cost of his life.

The woman next to him gasped in sudden recognition. "James?"

"Melissa? Matt!"

The familiar voice caused hope to spring into Matt's chest. Words died on his lips when he suddenly saw Justin bounding through the trees toward him. The sight of his friend forced a lump into his throat. The chubby man threw his arms around him. They held onto each other, neither one able to express the relief they felt. Emotionally exhausted, both men burst into tears.

"For false messiahs and false prophets will appear and perform great signs and wonders to deceive, if possible, even the elect."

Matthew 24:24

7

HERE IN MY GARDEN OF SHADOWS

They had tracked the retreating creatures as best as James could, but he didn't have the skills Mark had. Thinking of the old man made the boy's stomach churn. If he closed his eyes for more than the length of a blink he saw Mark crumple from his shot.

He had intentionally avoided the spot where his friend's body lay. He couldn't tell the others what he had done. He still felt cold and numb. He knew it was an accident, but would the others believe him? In his mind it was better if they thought the survivalist had been taken along with the priest or ran off on his own.

Nick tapped Matt on the shoulder as they made camp in a small clearing while dusk fell. "Our friends are long gone, mate."

Matt nodded. He seemed almost relieved to the Englishman. Elizabeth and Sean held hands when both realized that their search for Mark and Father Thomas was over. Ethan's head hung low as he rested with his back to a tree. Firmin warmed his hands next to a small fire he had brought to life.

Melissa took the news a little harder. "We can't just leave them out there all alone!"

"You know they're dead, right? Those things don't take prisoners! They musta' been a snack for the road!" James exploded.

The woman stared at the teenager. Her mouth was slowly opening and closing. Tears formed in her eyes and trickled down her cheeks. Matt rushed to her side and pulled her close to him. The former Marine shook his head at James.

"Don't be a dick." Sean levelled a steady gaze at his friend, "You don't have to be a dick about this."

"Seriously? You're telling me to play nice?" James pointed his finger at Sean, "It's the end of the world and you're worried about feelings? What in the fuck is wrong with you?"

"What the fuck is wrong with YOU?" Sean could feel a wave of anger rising in him as he glared at his friend. "This isn't about feelings. This isn't about the end of the world. This is about how you treat your friends. It's about not knowing what's going to happen next and who you can rely on to help you through it!"

"We all die! That's what happens next." James took a step towards Sean.

"Bullshit!" Matt stepped between the two kids before it could come to blows. "We've made it this far and we're still standing. As long as we stick together we'll be okay."

"Do you think Mark believed that? Or Father Murray?" Elizabeth's quiet voice cut through the rising tide of anger.

Everyone turned to the young woman. Her brown eyes held tears at their edges. She looked around at the small group, a sad smile creeping to her face. "I don't know if they did, but I do. I'd be dead if it wasn't for James and Sean. The three of us would be dead if it wasn't for Justin and Matt."

Catching on to what she was saying Nick nodded his head. "I'd be a goner if Sir Ethan hadn't shown up."

Justin looked at Matt for a moment then back to the group. "We all owe someone our life. We're all together here for a reason, even if that reason is something as simple as survival."

The former Marine cleared his throat. "We have a plan. We head to California. We avoid everyone that we can and stick to side roads as much as possible. We have to watch out for each other."

James crossed his arms and shook his head. "Like how we watched out for Mark? Or how these two watched out for Father Murray?"

"Yes." Justin responded without any hesitation, "Just like they watched out for us. Hell, they could both be dead right now because they took a bite for one of us or maybe they led the creatures away. We don't know what happened to them. Think about that!"

Matt raised his hands. "We've all had one hell of a day. Let's get some rest and figure out what our next move is in the morning."

Silence fell among the small group as they settled in for the night. The crackling of the fire melded peacefully with the other sounds of the forest. James rested on his side and watched the shadows created by the flames dancing among the trees. He didn't realize he was crying until the front of his shirt was soaked by his tears.

Firmin watched as James cried himself to sleep. The Frenchman sighed. He had grown quite fond of his surrogate family. He cared about each one of them even if he didn't understand what they said. He wanted to comfort the boy, but whatever the child was struggling with seemed to only let itself out when no one was watching. Looking at the increasingly smaller group of survivors he hoped the only monsters they saw in the future would be the ones in their minds. He just feared that the demons in his thoughts may be worse than the ones chasing them.

His temples throbbed with every beat of his heart. The rhythm of the pounding mixed with the tromping of several feet caused his stomach to churn in fear when he realized what he must be surrounded by. He opened his eyes only to immediately snap them shut again when the glaring light of the sun sent pain exploding in his skull.

Father Murray numbly felt the rough terrain scraping against his skin as he was lugged along the ground. His arms trailed out above his head as he struggled to find the strength to move them. His legs were lifted slightly; creating the proper angle for his current mode of travel. He could feel the sharp points of monstrous claws firmly anchored in the muscles of his legs. Every bump, every jostle sent tendrils of pain up the appendages. The smell of blood was strong in his nostrils. It took a few moments for his pain soaked mind to comprehend that the blood was his.

Taking a deep breath to prepare himself for the sting Thomas gingerly opened his eyes. Agony flared in his head once more. Queasiness replaced the fear in his stomach and he felt hot bile rise up in his throat. Turning to the side he spit it out. As he did, his predicament was verified. He was in the middle of a group of five creepers with the largest of them holding his legs.

The assemblage appeared to be made up of children between three and twelve. Clothing hung from their gaunt, greyish bodies in patches. Their small, bare feet seemed immune to the harsh floor of the forest. Not one of the creatures had so much as a scratch on it. That puzzled him at first until he remembered how fast the damn things healed.

As the troupe plowed along he could hear the rustling of underbrush being cleared out of the way. The stench from their unwashed bodies combining with his blood and the flora of the area created a thick, musty odor.

He allowed his head to roll back into place and stared up at the sky. The vast blueness was dotted by small clouds and were only obscured when tree limbs appeared above the trail he was being drug along. *I'm still in the woods. Why am I still in the woods? Why am I even still alive?*

He couldn't even remember clearly what had happened. One moment he was swinging Melissa's empty rifle at one of the hellish kids and the next he was being hauled along like luggage. *Where in the fuck are they taking me? Why did they keep me alive? I gotta' get away from these things!*

He closed his eyes and concentrated on clenching his hands

into fists. It took a few moments before the battered limbs responded. Once he felt he had regained enough control over them he looked for the right weapon. Father Murray dared a quick glance around. Several broken branches were within easy reach of him as well as a few good sized rocks.

His hands closed around a stone that held a jagged edge on one side. With all the strength he could gather he pulled his legs toward him and sat up with his make-shift weapon leading the way. Pain roared in his legs as the beasts claws were torn free from his skin. The demonic child fell back into his attack. The momentum helped bury the rock deep in its skull.

In a flash, Father Murray was on his feet running. Howls of rage erupted from the throats of the four remaining creepers as they bolted after him in pursuit. The quick exertion caused the fallen priest's head to pound even more. His vision blurred as a high pitched ringing sounded in his ears.

Every breath created a sharp sting on his right side. He hoped that during his capture a rib or two hadn't been broken. He weaved between trees as he ran. More than once he felt the rush of air as a clawed hand whistled past his head.

He shifted hard to the left grabbing a small tree to help him keep his balance. From the corner of his eye he watched as one of his pursuers lost its footing and tumbled to the ground in a wailing heap. He allowed himself a quick smile at the small victory.

As he raced around a larger tree something struck him heavily in his lower back. He hit the ground hard; his breath was blasted from his lungs. Whatever had hit him felt like it was still on top of him. He felt the hot, fetid breath of one of the abominations on the nape of his neck.

He flung himself on his back. He barely managed to bring his arms up in time to grab the wrists of the smallest creeper he had ever seen as it lashed out at him. The hell-child couldn't possibly be more than two years old. Soft, baby features had turned grey and gaunt. Cute, chubby baby hands were now elongated, ending in nasty talons.

The twisted creature screeched in his face. Thomas hurled the thing away from him and scampered backwards a few yards before regaining his footing. He turned quickly and bounced face first off a mountain of fetid flesh. Thomas stumbled back gagging. Before he could even register what he was staring at he was hoisted in the air.

The creature resembled a crazed weightlifting fanatic. Grey skin was stretched tightly over iron corded muscles cast on a six-and-a-half-foot-tall frame. The jawline jutted out and was filled with vicious needle-like teeth. Ragged blonde hair covered the head in small patches and a few stray hairs found their way over a sloped forehead. Deep blue eyes stared at him with unconcealed hatred as the monster held him out at arm's length.

With arms pinned at his sides he watched in horror as the smaller creature he had just tossed crawl up the leg of the creature holding him. It came to rest on the larger beasts shoulder. Both of the demonic hell-beasts continued to stare at him. Slowly, the smaller one crept down the left arm of the other until its twisted face nearly touched his.

He could hear more footsteps rushing towards him, but he couldn't break eye contact with the once innocent face in front of him. The small creeper screeched at him again. The piercing force of the sound sent the ringing in his ears to a high crescendo. He clamped his eyes shut as a wave of agony exploded in his head. All sound, all feeling flew away from him. For a brief moment he was terrified. Finally, trapped in the shadows of his mind, he allowed himself to be pulled down into the waiting darkness.

Thomas wasn't sure if it was the overpowering stench of decay or his aching body that woke him. He couldn't open his left eye. It felt puffy and bruised. His legs alternated between feeling numb and like they were burning. The rest of him throbbed, but thankfully the annoying ringing in his ears was gone. He took small breaths. The pain in his right side making anything more than the smallest intake of oxygen impossible.

It was night now. He was lying in the dirt on the forests floor. Only a small sliver of the moon was visible in the sky. Its light was barely enough to make out small forms that shuffled around him. He could hear the monsters well enough though. They made no effort in hiding their movements.

He made out the sounds of at least a dozen of the small ones scurrying around. So far he had not heard any trace of the large one that had captured him, nor had he seen the little one that accompanied the hulking beast.

The shuffling around him slowed until the only sound he could hear was the wind fluttering through the trees. The sudden push of air brought the odor of rotting meat to his nostrils. His stomach churned at the sickly sweet smell.

A wailing split the night as one of the children belted out a long yowl. Soon, the other hellish kids joined in. Fighting a wave of nausea Thomas forced his head to turn in the direction of the unholy howls.

Gaunt, child-sized figures were kneeling on the ground facing a building. The fallen priest could barely make out the outline of a porch attached to the silhouette of an old house. His eyes quickly focused on the source of the noxious scent. Piled around the structure were unmoving bodies. A soft, reddish light glowed faintly from inside. He watched in terror-filled fascination as the glow slowly moved from one room to another.

The chorus of wails grew louder. Soon it was accompanied by dirty hands and feet pounding on the dry ground. There was a marked rhythm to the thrashing. It was drum-like with a fast tempo. The demons were whipping themselves into a fury. No attention was being paid to him at all.

He cautiously attempted rolling on his side. Nearly swooning from the effort he collapsed in a quivering heap. He closed his good eye and took a few deeper breaths. The right side of his ribcage felt numb. His breathing grew labored. An abrupt coughing fit sent liquid fire through his lungs and trickles of blood spewing from his mouth. *Yep. Fuckin' ribs are busted.*

The clamor around him halted leaving only the wind to once again fill the deafening silence. A warm radiance washed over his face. Struggling, he managed to force both of his eyes open. Squatting next to him was one of the most beautiful young women he had ever seen.

Soft, blonde bangs rested just above her eyebrows as she smiled impishly at him through pouty lips. The curves of her braless breasts peaked out from the sides of the loose denim overall shorts she wore. The only thing that kept him from being aroused was the unnatural red glow emanating from her eyes.

She reached out and gently rubbed a soft, velvety hand down his cheek until she cupped his chin in her hands. She wiped the coppery liquid from his lips with her thumb. She pulled her hand away and slowly brought it up to her mouth. She playfully sucked on her blood covered digit while staring at him.

"You taste bitter. Why, you're worse than coffee boiled in piss. Do you know that?" She spat on the ground next to his face.

Father Murray stared blankly at her. A cold chill started in his hands and feet and worked its way through the rest of his body. His vision started to get blurry. He blinked his eyes several times to refocus them on her.

"It's the sinning, you know. All of that evil inside is just tendering you up. It makes you taste good to them." She motioned toward the gathered monsters, "They'll savor every bite. Every scream you make will just be more seasoning for their steak, so to speak."

She straddled him gently. Her petite body barely placed any pressure against his. She leaned closer to him until their faces nearly touched. "It doesn't have to be like that for you. In fact," she slid her hand down between his legs. "It can feel pretty good if you listen to me."

Thomas had a hard time grasping anything she was saying. He knew that he was dying. His lungs were punctured, most likely from his ribcage. He had lost a lot of blood from the gashes in his legs. His head still hurt like hell. His vision gradually started to cloud over.

"Look at you. Just driftin' away like it's an afternoon nap. Oh, you poor thing. Here, let me make it all better."

Her voice sounded muffled, like she was talking through a tin can at him. He felt both of her hands resting on the back of his head, her thumbs nestling along his cheeks. His sight failed him and everything went black. He vaguely felt moist, hot lips being placed against his forehead.

His vision returned in an explosion of red. He gasped and took in a huge lungful of air as something like an electric shock flooded his entire body. He could taste blood in his mouth, but felt no pain from his right side… or anywhere. The numbness that had crept over him retreated in the face of a warm tingling sensation flowing throughout his limbs.

The young blonde with the red glowing blue eyes was once again kneeling next to him. The fallen priest sat up and stared at her slack-jawed. She smiled at him. Her pouty lips puffed out slightly as she ran her tongue over them.

His gaze was so fixated on the woman that he had forgotten about the mob of creatures that surrounded him until the small creeper from his earlier encounter jumped on her shoulder like a pet monkey. He scuttled backward a few yards before a tree intercepted him.

"What are you?"

She stood and took a step toward him. "Why, I'm just a poor helpless girl struggling to make it in this crazy world."

He instinctively shoved her away. "Bullshit. No games. What are you?"

Her eyes flared. The reddish glow encompassed the area surrounding him and sent the creature on her shoulder jumping away with a shriek. "I'd think you'd be more grateful to the lady who just saved your life, priest."

Thomas leaned against the tree staring up at the mysterious woman. All around her small beasts were hissing at him. They looked up at her as if asking for permission to attack him. She crossed her arms under her breasts. The casual act exposed more of them from the top of her overalls. Her soft, young face was twisted in snarl as she glared down at him.

He could feel a thick cloud of palpable evil emanating from her. He took a deep breath and gently let it out of his newly restored lungs. "You're right. That was very rude of me. Thank you."

Her face slowly lost its scowl. "That's better. Now maybe we can talk like civilized folk."

One of the creepers scampered next to her and leaned its head against her thigh. She absently began stroking its head. Father Murray glanced nervously at the creature. Noticing where his gaze was concentrated she smiled at him again.

"Oh, don't mind my little friends. They won't say anything about our conversation."

She held her hand out to him. He tentatively grasped it. With a strength not possible for such a small frame, she pulled him to his feet in front of her. He towered over her by at least ten inches, but her presence still overwhelmed him.

"Why am I still alive?"

"Right to the point, I like that. Why do you think you're still alive, Thomas?"

"How do you know my name? Have we met?" Thomas's mind was reeling trying to place the woman.

She laughed. It was musical sounding. "I just healed all yer' ills, including that pesky prostate cancer that had just started formin' earlier this year and yer' surprised I know yer' name?"

The fallen priest stood gaping at her. *She has a point.* "Fair enough, I guess. Zombie kids, end of the world… why the hell not throw in a faith-healer?"

"Call me Dea. Now, go ahead and answer yer' own question."

"I'm alive because you need me for something."

"Handsome *and* smart. Good answer. Care to be adventurous and guess why?"

He stood silent for a moment as his brain raced through a list of possibilities. His eyes caught the pile of corpses. "You want me to bring people to you."

"Swing and a miss, but not a bad guess. I want you to tell me everything you know about Sean Tyler."

The interior condition of the cabin was no better than the outside. The paint-pealed walls were splattered in large patches of mold. The couch and once plush chair in the small living room had large gashes ripped into the fabric. They were also wet to the touch. The thought of what may have caused the moisture made Thomas' stomach churn and was the reason he was sitting on the floor.

After he had finished telling the woman about Sean she leaned back in the couch and closed her eyes. That was more than an hour ago and she had yet to respond or make any other movement. He stared at her. He couldn't keep his eyes from wandering over her body. He readily admitted to himself that she turned him on, but he was also more afraid of her than any of the beasts that he had seen in this new world.

Rotting floorboards creaked and popped as Thomas adjusted his position for what seemed liked the hundredth time. Movement on the porch reminded him just how tenuous his place in the grand scheme of things had become.

He was in the middle of the woods surrounded on all sides by monsters from mankind's worst nightmares. It was taking every ounce of willpower he had not to go stark raving mad. Unsettled was not a strong enough word to describe the feeling that flowed over his nerves. He couldn't stare out of the windows anymore. Every time he had looked up he had been greeted by the sight of creepers peering into the house.

"That isn't as helpful as I'd hoped."

The unexpected sound of Dea's voice caused Thomas to jerk. His attention snapped from her tits back to her face. She was smiling at him, the red glow made her face look soft and vulnerable. He felt his face flush. He looked away from her. By chance, he glanced out the window for just a moment. It was long enough to watch one of the hell-children take a bite out of a severed arm.

"Why are these staying small? I was told by one of my former group that the child-zombies were growing into adults really fast."

"They stay like this because I want them to. They do what I say. They are my children."

He swung his head back around. The young woman was still smiling at him. The situation seemed outlandish. A quick burst of laughter escaped him. The woman's smile grew even wider. He laughed harder. He couldn't help himself. Laughter boomed out of him until his sides ached and tears rolled down his face.

"Am… Ha! Am… I goin' crazy? Ha! HA!" Thomas snorted out the words between fits of hysterical laughter.

Her smile slowly eased from her face. She licked her lips and stood up. She pushed him down on his back and slid on top of him. "Crazy? Oh no. Crazy would be easy. The only place yer' goin' to is Hell, Father."

He continued to laugh as she unbuttoned the overalls she wore. Pink nipples sprang erect as denim fell away from them. She pulled his hands up and placed them on her breasts. She slowly started to grind against him. His laughter faded as he became aroused.

She leaned down and kissed him. She tasted like ashes. Her hands rubbed his chest as she moaned in his ear. She stood up and peeled away the rest of her clothing. Reaching down she lifted him as easily as if he was an infant. His fear caused him to be more turned on.

She tossed him on the couch. He hastily undid his pants and yanked them off. She climbed on top and guided him into her. She moaned louder as she felt him quivering and thrusting under her. It was over in a few moments. Thomas let out a loud hiss as he came deep inside of her.

She stayed on him for a few seconds licking his ear and kissing him. She finally rolled away and stretched in pleasure. They sat on the couch and stared at each other. She slid closer to him and laid her head in his lap looking up at him.

"So Hell is real? I really hate to hear that." Father Murray murmured as he tussled her blonde hair in his hand.

"Try to look on the bright side, Thomas." She turned over and took him in her mouth. She sucked on him until he was rock hard again. She continued to use her mouth and tongue and brought him to another powerful orgasm.

She sat up and licked her lips. The fallen priest was breathing hard as he stared at her naked body. "That is a bright side."

"Yep and I'll keep fucking and sucking you as long as you do what I say. So long as you play this game with me."

"What game?"

"Why, any game I want."

"Fair enough."

Thomas knelt in front of her and buried his face between her legs.

"So our elders and all the inhabitants of our country spoke to us, saying, "Take provisions in your hand for the journey, and go to meet them and say to them, We are your servants; now then, make a covenant with us. This our bread was warm when we took it for our provisions out of our houses on the day that we left to come to you; but now behold, it is dry and has become crumbled. These wineskins which we filled were new, and behold, they are torn; and these our clothes and our sandals are worn out because of the very long journey."

Joshua 9:11-13

LONDON BRIDGE IS FALLING DOWN

As the miles continued to roll away behind them Justin began to feel better physically than he could ever remember. His pants were so loose that he had to make new holes in his belt and his shirt hung off him. Three weeks of walking had done him and the rest of the small group some good.

By his estimation they had covered a little over five hundred miles since the creeper attack had brought both groups together. That was five hundred miles closer to California. Whatever the hell that meant. Justin understood the reasoning behind heading for a more hospitable climate. It was only the second week of September, but the weather was getting colder and he didn't think they would be making it before the first snow came down.

The only reason they had managed such good time was because of a truck they had found. The old Ford was in good condition, and had a full tank of gas. That helped them plod through some back roads and got them almost out of Kansas before they got mired down in mud.

Kansas had not been easy walking. Even though the terrain was nice and level the downside was they could see for miles in any direction. This meant they could be easily spotted. Matt suggested they try to keep as low to the ground as possible while moving. The group was soon complaining about sore backs from walking hunched over to throw less of a silhouette against the plains.

The usually stoic Ethan grumbled loudest about the plan once it was set in motion. His tall, gangly frame had more strain put on it from the heavy armor he wore. At the end of the first day of marching through Kansas his back was going into spasms. Firmin had massaged his muscles until the worst of it passed. Ethan hoped he had made his gratitude known to the Frenchman through smiles and hugs.

They had been making camp without building fires and got by eating cold, canned food. The last couple of days saw a drastic drop in temperature, and they were doubling up under blankets for added warmth.

As night fell and the temperatures dropped again they decided to risk a fire. The small one they built barely offered any warmth to the chill of the wind. The group sat huddled around the tiny flames using blankets and sleeping bags to hide the glow as best they could on the plains.

"What happens when the wood runs out?" Melissa cuddled closer to Matt.

"We can find other things to burn. The Indians and settlers used manure. I'm sure we can find some shit around here somewhere." Matt laughed weakly.

"We need to find a town. We need to find heavier clothing and blankets or we're all gonna' end up freezing to death." James's voice killed any mirth remaining after Matt's shit joke.

"The kid's right, mate," Nick sighed. "We could do with a bit of a supply run. Maybe find another auto with keys inside or a fuckin' book at the library on how to hotwire a fucker."

"And we can grab a French to English dictionary!" Ethan chimed in. He patted Firmin on the back, "How does that sound, bud?"

Firmin smiled meekly and held his hands out. "J'espère

que vous dites que nous allons construire un feu plus grand demain. Mes couilles sont froides."

"See, Firmin agrees!" Ethan laughed.

Sean and Elizabeth were wrapped under the same blanket. They had paid little attention to the conversation going on around them until they heard the Frenchman speak.

"So what's the plan?" Elizabeth asked.

Matt looked around the small group. "Tomorrow I'll scout out the first town we come to."

"You mean 'we'll' scout it out." Justin corrected.

"No. I mean me. I'll take a look. I've done this kind of thing before in the Marines. I've been trained."

"Wait a tic, mate. I don't like the idea of you wanderin' out amongst Hell's finest all by yer' lonesome." Nick argued.

"Neither do I!" Melissa cocked her head to the side and glared at him.

"He's the only one that can do it," Sean's quiet voice was nearly overpowered by a sudden crackling in the fire. "Ethan makes a ton of noise, Firmin wouldn't understand anything Matt said, and Nick just sticks out like a sore thumb. Justin, you are still too out of shape to pull something like this off."

"What about me?" Melissa crossed her arms under her breasts and stared at the kid.

"He likes you a lot. He would be more worried about you than his own safety. That's the same reason he won't take me, James, or Liz."

"Sean nailed it. Out of everyone here Nick would be the only one I would even consider bringing. Sorry, Justin." Matt shrugged at his friend.

"I understand, but you're taking him then. None of us need to run off alone." The former pastor poked the fire with a small branch of wood.

"I'll be happy to tag along. What's a holiday without exploring the local culture?" Nick smiled.

"Okay wildman, but we've got to do something about the hair. People can see that—"

"Out of the fuckin' equation, mate. It isn't gettin' cropped," Nick gruffly interrupted. "I'll tuck these lovely locks down the back of my jacket."

The finality and vehemence in his tone set everyone back. The Englishmen's typically jovial features had developed a sudden scowl. His eyes narrowed and his jaw clenched. None of the group had seen him react this way to anything.

"Ummm... sure. Okay... yeah. That'll work I guess," Matt didn't press him any further. "It's settled then. The next town we come across me and Nick will grab some shit while the rest of you hunker down and wait for us to get back."

None of the other kids cared that he was sick. They didn't understand that the operations he went through would take time to heal his scalp. All they were concerned about in primary was how different he was.

They mocked him. They shoved him. They threw anything they could pick up at him. Even the teachers were laughing and pointing. He climbed a tree to get away from them, but that wasn't enough. The more nimble of his peers scampered up after him, forcing him to jump to the ground and flee the school.

As he ran from the playground, they chased him. The sky darkened and lightning flashed through the clouds. Behind him, the taunts of children turned into demonic cackles. Looking over his shoulder he saw his former classmates twisting into grey-skinned beasts with razor sharp teeth.

His teachers were growing larger. They were becoming heavily muscled and twisting into demonic bipedal forms. Each of them had necrotic skin dropping off by the pound only to be quickly replaced by new tissue. They gave chase alongside their smaller counterparts.

He was carrying a guitar now. He couldn't remember picking it up. He played as he ran. He felt himself growing taller; growing up. He played the instrument harder and harder until his fingers started to bleed. Applause erupted all around him from creepers as they stopped to lap at blood that fell from his hands.

Nick ran. He passed buildings that were falling down from neglect. He tromped over busted asphalt as he headed to the town limits. He thought he was safe when he made it out of town, until he came to a collapsed bridge over a river of blood.

He could still hear the beasts behind him closing in. Thunder exploded all around him. Seeing no other choice Nick jumped into the river. The blood was warm. It clung to him. The thickness of the liquid made swimming hard. His head went under and his mouth filled with the fluid. He surfaced sputtering, trying to clear himself of the coppery taste.

He fought with his clothes. His leather jacket and heavy boots were dragging him down. He struggled to remove the encumbering items from his body. After going under a few more times he finally managed to rid himself of the jacket. With the weight of it off him, swimming became more manageable.

He reached the far shore gasping for breath. His arms and legs ached from the exertion of the swim. He wrung the viscous fluid from his hair as best he could. Storm clouds still raged overhead. Lightning caught his attention and he looked up in time to see a horde of the monstrous creepers diving into the river.

He stumbled away from the river's edge and down a dirt road, away from the approaching horde. He coughed as he walked. With each hack more blood was expelled from his lungs. He was starting to get used to the taste.

The clouds above finally unleashed their furry. Torrents of rain soaked the ground, but not a single droplet landed on him. Mud mired him down. Each step ended with a loud sucking sound as he pulled his feet from the sludge. A cold wind swept over his body causing him to shiver and regret the loss of his jacket even more. Over the roar of thunder he could still hear the maniacal laughter of demonic kids getting closer to him.

He yanked the blood-soaked boots off his feet and tossed them aside. Without them, he moved easily through the muck. The storm lessened and he once again found himself on dry ground. The dirt road soon gave way to gravel. On each side of him was a thick hedge of plants with sharp needles.

The rocks cut painfully into his feet. He walked for what seemed like miles, each step more agonizing than the last. He considered heading back to get his boots, but when he turned he saw a veritable army of monsters of all sizes. They were following the trail left by his bloody footprints.

He started running. He ignored all the flashes of pain from his feet as best he could. The walls of thorns grew higher, but slowly opened up beyond the road. Soon he was in a clearing with a small white house that had a wrap-around porch. He could smell fresh baked bread coming from the open windows. He saw birds on the lawn and could hear more chirping from the back of the building.

He stepped on the stairs leading up to the porch. He stopped when they creaked. The front door opened and a beautiful, young red-headed woman stepped outside. She wore a pink flowered print dress and black sandals. Nick gaped up at her. She looked familiar, but he couldn't place from where. He was stunned to see anyone look so clean and vibrant in such a nasty world.

A screech from behind caused him to spin around. At the edge of the lawn were five creepers. One of them was missing its lower right leg and crawled along the ground toward them. The Englishmen bolted up the few remaining steps and flung his arm around the woman's waist dragging her screaming inside.

He pushed her towards a couch. She lost her footing and landed heavily on the cushions. He slammed the door and slid the deadbolt into place. Breathing heavily he rested his head against the door for a moment.

"We need to barricade the windows. Do you have any—"

He was hoisted in the air and flung head over heels against the wall. He crashed to the ground in a daze, unable to catch his breath. The woman he had just saved was on top of him and changing right before his eyes. Her small frame expanded as muscles bulged. Her skin and flowery dress ripped away while the woman screamed.

Nick dully watched as the creature lifted both arms above its head. As they came crashing down a loud CRACK from outside the house sent the monster's head violently spinning to the side. Half of the beast's skull erupted and it toppled off of him.

Nick stood on trembling legs as more gunshots went off outside. He crept toward the window shrinking with each step.

He was a child again when he peered outside. His classmates stood shoulder to shoulder with the grey-skinned demons.

Laughter erupted from all of them as they pointed at him. He covered his ears with his hands and turned away from the window in tears. The large beast was now sitting in the middle of the living room. Dressed now only in tattered rags of a once beautiful dress; it raised a mighty hand, pointed, and laughed. The echoing of the sound through the missing part of its skull created a wheezing as blood spurted from the wound.

Nick sprang towards the rear of the house, but lost his footing as the ground trembled. He scampered across the wood floor as the trembling increased. He felt strong hands clamp around his shoulders. He screamed as the house rocked on its foundation and the floor fell away.

"Nick!"

Ethan's harsh whisper cut through his nightmare. He felt himself being shaken. He opened his eyes to see his friend kneeling next to him on the ground.

"I'm awake… Fuck off with the shaking, mate!" The rocker sat up and sniffed through his nose heavily.

"You were moaning and thrashing around."

"Yeah, no surprise. Monsters out here. Monsters in my head. Monsters every fuckin' where."

Nick looked around rapidly blinking his eyes to clear them. Matt and Melissa were snoozing away. Firmin was wrapped tightly in a blanket and lay shivering next to the remains of the fire. Sean and Elizabeth were sharing a sleeping bag. James lay on his back with only the tip of his nose exposed from his sleeping roll. Justin was tossing and turning, but not too loudly. Ethan was the only other person awake.

"Nightmares are a blast aren't they? What was it? Were you naked in school?"

Nick flinched. "Something like that, mate. I gotta' piss."

The Englishmen stumbled away from camp and relieved himself. He took deep, steady breaths of the chill air to calm himself. He stretched and yawned. As he was about to head back to Ethan a soft glow in the distance caught his eye. He blinked a few more times and tried to focus on the source.

The light didn't appear to be moving. He couldn't make out anything around it. He also had no way of knowing just how far off it was on the Kansas plains. He looked back and saw Ethan keeping a watchful gaze on him. He motioned for the lanky giant to join him.

"What is it?" Ethan whispered when he got closer.

"Some kind of light I think. Maybe a town, but who the fuck can tell?"

"Yeah, I think it is. It looks like the road we've been shadowing leads right to it."

Nick rested a hand on his chin and made a clicking noise a few times with his mouth. "So that's a right proper start for a search when we get to it."

Ethan shrugged and continued staring off into the distance. "Man, just... Just be careful when you get there."

"Don't worry about ole' Nick, Sir Ethan. Me an' Matt won't be long at all."

"Light means people. Don't laugh when I say this, but I've seen enough movies to know how they're goin' to react to others. So, be fucking careful. I mean it." Ethan's tone was calm and measured.

"Look mate, I admit I've never done anything like this before. Truth be told I don't even know the first or second fuckin' thing on how to go about it, but something tells me Military Matt has a clue. I'll follow his lead and we'll both be right as the fuckin' mail."

Ethan looked at the rocker and grinned. "Military Matt? That's the best you could come up with? Really? Man, that's so lame."

"Okay, Sir Ethan. What do you call the fucka'?"

"I call him Private Prick. Not because I think he's an asshole, he's not, but he's definitely pricking Melissa with something each night."

Nick nodded. He chuckled and cuffed his young friend across the shoulder. The metal on his leather gloves made a *ting* as they connected with the chainmail Ethan wore. The first rays of morning greeted them as they turned around.

Together they walked back in to camp.

"I will destine you for the sword, and all of you will fall in the slaughter; for I called but you did not answer, I spoke but you did not listen. You did evil in my sight   and chose what displeases me."

Isaiah 65:12

IT FOLLOWED HER TO SCHOOL ONE DAY

On the outskirts of town they found an old blue barn with a tin roof and peeling paint to wait in until nightfall. It was surrounded by unharvested wheat left to rot. The smell reminded the group of stale beer.

Matt and the Englishmen left just as dusk settled in with Justin in tow. Matt had reluctantly agreed to take the former pastor with them only on the condition he play the role of look out from a safe distance away.

An hour after they had scurried off into the darkness Firmin was pacing uneasily back and forth inside the barn. His route took him past all four windows on the ground floor. He would take a few moments to peer outside from each one, keeping an eye out for Matt and Nick's return.

He could hear Sean and Elizabeth moving around in the loft above him. James was most likely still positioned where he had last seen him; at the window facing the town the others had ran off to with rifle in hand. Ethan and Melissa spoke quietly with each other as they reclined against the walls of a stall.

Firmin softly chuckled at himself for the hundredth time since he had ran off and left his French to English dictionary on the bus. Grunts and gestures only went so far after all. He was frustrated to no end that he couldn't communicate verbally, but he did try to find humor in his own personal situation.

He didn't find anything funny about the state of the world though. Looking out one of the windows he couldn't suppress a sigh. Wasted wheat, overgrown vegetation, and hopelessness surrounded them all. Firmin had always been overly cheery in his outlook, but even his indomitable positivity was suffering.

He pulled a small block of partially carved wood from his pocket and went to work on it with his knife. His experienced hands feeling for what the oak told him it wanted to be. He carved and whittled away as he walked, hardly looking at his work.

Ethan and Melissa continued with their conversation. Firmin stopped and listened. There were no other sounds coming from the barn. Sean and Elizabeth must have fallen asleep or were being *very* quiet at something. *Ahhhh jeune amour.* He smiled at the thought and went back to work on his carving.

"Okay… so if it *was* the Rapture why are you still here? What makes you a bad person?"

Ethan was taken back by the blunt question. Melissa and him had been talking about the events that led up to their current situation. When he had casually mentioned that Justin had said the Rapture had come and it was God's judgement to let hell walk on Earth while the faithful were called home. He hadn't expected her to react the way she had.

A scowl covered her face and she set her jaw tightly. She clenched her hands into fists and rubbed them together a few times before unclenching them and crossing her arms under her breasts. Her mask of anger slipped for a moment and Ethan thought she looked ashamed about something. Then the mask came back up and she had barked the question at him.

"Well, if it is the biblical God… What *doesn't* make me a bad person is a better question. I'm sure I've committed every sin except murder."

"I'm being serious!"

"Me too."

"Ugh!" She tossed her hands in the air.

"Hear me out," Ethan sighed. "We're supposed to ask for forgiveness, right? Admit what we've done and truly be sorry and repent. Then we have to change our lives and do our best to never do the same thing again."

"Okay. And…?" Melissa had her arms crossed again.

"And how many times have you done that? Hell, I can say I don't know if I ever have. So that means I am in no way following any of the Christian rules or doctrines." Ethan shrugged his shoulders sending thousands of metal rings clinking against one another.

Melissa glared at him. "The news said it was a new strain of virus. That people's skin was turning red and they got some kind of sores all over their bodies, like boils or something. How can that be the Rapture?"

The lanky young man shook his head. "I don't know, but, how did it hit every kid in the world? How did it knock them all out at about the same time? How do you explain the large ones? No… A virus my ass. This was something bigger. This was something that turned people into monsters. Something that turned people against each other on a larger scale than anything in history. Only God could do that."

Melissa shook her head. She had gone to church on a regular basis. She prayed. She tried to do good things for people. She couldn't except that if the Rapture had happened she hadn't made the cut. Not so much for her own sake, but because the thought of Dylan not being good enough for Heaven was a thought she couldn't bear.

"What about Father Murray and Justin? Why weren't they given a golden ticket to Heaven?" She smirked.

"Well Father Murray *is* Catholic so—"

"Ugh! Be serious!"

"From what Sean and Matt have said there was something

off about Tom. Sean always felt uneasy around him and Matt outright hated the man."

"Matt never mentioned that to me." Melissa's mouth formed a small frown.

"Maybe he doesn't want to speak ill of the dead. As far as Justin goes," Ethan shrugged and shook his head. "He had a meltdown when he found his fiancé cheating on him and damn near beat the guy to death. Then he turned into an alcoholic, so there's that. Something tells me he hasn't been in the mood to talk to God for a while."

"So what now? If this is the end of days why are we even trying?" Melissa felt angry tears forming in her eyes. "And why didn't he take Sean, James, and Elizabeth?"

"I don't have any answers. I honestly have no idea what happened. The idea of this being biblically apocalyptic is the only thing keeping me sane, and, yes, I know how crazy that sounds. I just can't find anything else that can explain it."

Melissa and Ethan sat in silence. The only sounds in the barn were from Firmin as his knife whittled away to the beat of his footsteps and the wind as it whistled through the cracks of the boards. Melissa shivered as an especially cold gust wracked her to the bone.

"Maybe you're right," Melissa flung her arms around the young man in a desperate hug. "Maybe God did do this and we all deserve to die."

Ethan held his arms out wide for a moment before wrapping them around the distraught woman. He held her close for a few seconds then smiled. "Just to show how right you are; feeling your tits against my stomach is turning me on right now."

Melissa burst into laughter through her tears and slapped him playfully on his back. "Pervert!"

"Yep, that's me. What a great example of why the human race needs exterminated." Ethan joined in the laughter as he let her go.

Firmin shyly walked up and hugged Melissa. He took her hands and pressed something into her palms. "Ne pleure pas. Tant que nous vivons il ya de l'espoir. Espoir et raisons de sourire."

She looked down and saw she was holding a magnificent carving of a horse. She smiled and hugged the Frenchman one more time. Firmin's face was blushing red when she pulled away. He nodded at her and gave three little waves as he continued his self-appointed patrol route, whistling softly.

"And he's a great example of why the human race needs saved," She whispered. "I wonder why he's still here."

James rested his rifle on top of the hay bale he had drug under the window. He scanned the terrain for any signs of movement. So far he had counted seventeen rabbits, three deer, and one armadillo. He let his binoculars fall away from his face. They were caught by their strap and bounced against his chest. He stretched and yawned. He was never very good at waiting under the best of conditions. Now, being on such edge made it almost impossible for him. His friends had been gone for a little over two hours and each minute seemed like an eternity.

He could hear Sean and Elizabeth at the other end of the loft making out in the hay. He smirked remembering how far he had gotten with her. He had a feeling it was a lot further than Sean. He was still pissed that she had threatened to deny the whole thing if it ever came up. She had said she didn't want to hurt Sean's feelings because she never told him. *What about my feelings?*

He risked a quick glance in their direction. He was disappointed to find that they had moved around the pile of hay and out of his view. The only thing he saw was an old wooden ladder propped up against the wall. He wouldn't have minded a good skin show. As far as Liz and Sean went he was happy for them. He didn't have any strong feelings about the girl, but he was jealous that Sean was getting some action and he wasn't.

Grudgingly he lifted his binoculars and turned to look out the window again. Laughter drifted up from below him. He gritted his teeth. The whole point of hiding was to not be found.

Melissa had been turning more and more into an emotional wreck over the last couple of weeks. He knew she was worried about her kid, but emotion wasn't going to get them to California any faster. Her nervous laughter was happening more often and just showed him that she was slipping further into a depression.

A softly whistled tune crept up as well. *Firmin, God damn it!* The Frenchmen wasn't the loudest of the issues downstairs and the wind probably overpowered the sound anyway. James just didn't have a clue how good the zombie's sense of hearing was. None of them did.

Zombies. He knew they were zombies. No matter how hard everyone else tried to come up with an explanation, or name, he just knew what they were. They healed so damn fast you had to get them in the head to put one down. *Isn't that the biggest requisite to be a zombie in the first place?*

The memory of Mark suddenly slammed into him. It had been a few days since he had thought of the old man. It was a record for his guilt ridden mind. He let the binoculars fall again. A lump swelled in his throat. He found himself staring at the rifle on the bale of hay in front of him. He knew he could place the barrel under his chin and with one quick jerk of his finger there would be no more pain.

He shook the thought away. It hadn't been the first time he had entertained the notion of suicide. During the last week his head had been filled with all kinds of dark ideas concerning self-harm. He wasn't afraid to die. He already had come to the realization that all of them were going to bite it. If not today, maybe tomorrow; if not tomorrow next week. If not next week... sometime soon. Everyone was already dead. They were just going through the motions of living. Himself included.

He started to feel a dull pain in his temples. His face flushed. He started sweating; the combination of moisture and cold wind caused him to shiver. He placed a blanket over his jacket and held it tightly against his chest.

After a few minutes he felt better. These fits happened each time he let his guard down and entertained the ramblings going on in his head. He shrugged off the blanket. Lifting the binoculars, he concentrated on his sentry duties.

Sean felt blood pounding in his head; pumping through every vein in his body. Elizabeth's kisses and light caresses were sending his hormones into overdrive. They had been making out for at least a half hour and both of them were quivering and shaking. He was afraid to go too far too fast with her. His fear was the only thing keeping his hands in respectful places on her body.

She shifted in the hay pulling him closer to her. He wrapped his arms around her and took a deep breath to get his urges under control. He was relieved and disappointed at the same time that she didn't coax him on. He took a few more deep breaths through his nose. A faint, odd scent caught his attention. There was something familiar about it he couldn't place.

Elizabeth giggled as he climbed on top of her. She quieted as he continued past her poking around in the hay. She lay still for a moment in confusion then rolled on her stomach. She leaned on an elbow resting her head in her hand and smiled.

"Did you drop a condom?" She whispered playfully.

Sean continued to spread hay away from the pile. If he heard what she said he made no indication of it. He stopped for moment and sat back on his heels. In a flurry of motion he flung himself forward and dug into the pile with fury, tossing hay in every direction.

The young lady bit her tongue as she pulled hay out of her hair. She tossed it casually aside until she noticed some had dark brown splotches on them. She looked closer at where Sean was digging. More and more of the hay straws were discolored.

She saw movement from the corner of the pile. She held her breath as a large grey rat bolted from the hay. Another one soon followed, then another. She watched as several rats fled from Sean's manic digging.

A sharp intake of breath from her boyfriend caused her to turn back towards him. He was on his knees. He had his mouth covered with his right hand and was looking at her. He was shaking his head 'no' and pointed toward the ladder that led down to the ground floor. Puzzled, she looked in front of him. She couldn't stop the scream that erupted from her.

The headless corpse of a naked woman lay half exposed. The wood had soaked up much of the blood and the hay around it absorbed its fair share as well. Her side was busted open exposing half-eaten organs and intestines. A lone remaining rat greedily continued its meal. Piercing black eyes stared at the two of them daring them to try to take its feast.

Ethan and Firmin scampered up into the loft with weapons in hand before the girl had even finished screaming. James had no reaction when he leapt to investigate the girl's cry and spotted the body. He casually kicked the rat sending it flying through the air shrieking while Sean guided a sobbing Elizabeth toward the ladder.

Ethan took a step back when he saw the source of the commotion. Firmin knelt down and moved more hay out of the way without hesitation. With the body fully exposed he let out a low moan. The Frenchman examined the remaining portion of the neck. After a few moments he looked up at Ethan. His eyes were glazed over and his usually cheery face was devoid of emotion. He pointed at a spot in the wood that had a deep chunk cut out. He drug his forefinger along his throat then made a chopping motion with the same hand. Her head had been chopped off; most likely with an axe. A person had done this.

Ethan nodded his understanding and gripped the shotgun he carried tightly. It was bad enough knowing that demons had come to kill them all, but being so starkly reminded that humans have always been monsters sent a chill up his spine. He had no way of knowing for sure, but the lack of clothes on her almost surely meant that she had been violated before the brutal murder.

The kind-hearted giant pointed at the body and then made a digging motion with his arms. Firmin nodded. The pair of them searched in and around the barn for a shovel. When they couldn't find one they tried using a broken rake. The ground was too hard. Without proper tools it was impossible for them to dig into the cold earth. Reluctantly, Ethan and Firmin returned to the loft to pile more hay on top of the body.

While the two men worked on covering the corpse Melissa did her best to console Elizabeth. The poor girl was almost catatonic and only nodded dully at the woman's attempts at conversation. She kept her head rigid and stared straight in front of her. The only time she looked anywhere else was when she heard the pile of hay being shifted again above her.

Sean sat with James at the window his friend had been keeping watch from. The pair were scanning the area for any signs that someone, or something, had heard the girl's scream. So far the only movement that had caught their attention was a lone deer sprinting through a moonlit field.

"That must have killed the mood real quick, eh?" James whispered to the other boy.

Sean set his binoculars on the hay bail in front of him and glared at James. His angry gaze sliced through any mirth his friend thought he created with the snide comment. Sean clenched his hands together to keep from striking his friend.

"Why would you even say that?" Sean's face flushed as he hissed through clenched teeth.

"I was just trying to lighten the tension a little." James shrugged.

"Are you serious? How in the fuck could that 'lighten the tension' even a little bit?"

"I don't know, man… I just thought," James sighed and looked back out the window. "Hell, I just thought it would be funny."

Sean felt the anger slowly leave him as he stared fixedly at the older boy. James' expression was hard to read. There was no smirk or any hint of sarcasm. It was almost as if there was no emotion at all. It was like looking into the face of his father.

The wind picked up speed. It whistled through the barn between the cracks in the old wood before dying out to a low, soft moan. The rattling of metal from behind them drew his thoughts from his family.

"Why don't you two go on downstairs and get some rest. I can keep an eye out for 'em." Ethan's speech was slower than usual.

"I'm fine up here." James didn't even turn around.

"Thanks. I'll go check on Elizabeth and make sure she's okay." Sean picked his rifle up and with one last look at his troubled friend headed for the ladder.

Firmin carefully sorted through the hay in the stall and then piled it into a makeshift bed. He stretched out on it feeling each individual strand massaging his back. He pulled the woolen blanket he had found in the corner up to his chin and snuggled against it. If it wasn't for the high chance of being killed and eaten by hellish children it was almost like the sleepovers he had at his cousin's farm when he was a child.

He watched as shadows slowly took over the barn from the retreating moonlight. He tried to get the image of the decapitated woman from his mind, but his thoughts turned to imagining what she may have looked like. She was a blonde. The soft looking patch of hair between her legs had given him that much information.

Were her eyes blue? Maybe green? Were her lips soft and plump? Was her voice musical? What would her tongue have looked like nailed to a tree? He shook the thought away. It had been a long time since his urges had made him do… that.

He had spent so long repressing his desires he had almost been able to forget the things he had done, but to see such beautiful work laid bare before him was more than he could handle. Try as he might he couldn't get the image of the headless, naked form out of his mind. He could feel sweat forming on his brow as blood rushed to his face.

How many people have I killed? Thirty? Thirty-five? All of them so unique, yet they somehow blur together. He clamped his eyes shut and slowed his breathing. He vaguely remembered a brown haired hitchhiker he had picked up. The man had been friendly enough and was very entertaining. He couldn't remember what triggered it, but one moment they were laughing and joking then the next he had cut off his legs and driven an iron rebar spike through the foot of one of the detached limbs and into his victim's head.

He opened his eyes and stared at the darkness above him. He didn't know why he had done it. It just seemed like the right thing to do at the time. He knew he was different from everyone else. He knew he was sick; knew he needed help. The thought of him, or anything, hurting one of his friends was so abhorrent a few days ago that it turned his stomach, but seeing the body upstairs had stirred the darkness in him again.

He tried to calm his mind. His thoughts drifted to what the body upstairs would look like with Melissa's head on its shoulders. The thought pounded in his head. A ringing in his ears consumed him until he couldn't take it anymore. He slowly stood and peered over the wall into the next stall where the woman was sleeping. He watched the rise and fall of her chest. A few strands of hair fell across her face. They danced back and forth as they got caught in her breath. He rested his chin on the wall of the stall. He smiled down at her while she slumbered.

He couldn't remember pulling his knife from its sheath. It seemed to have just magically appeared in his hand. The blade reflected what little light there was in the barn along its edge. Firmin's attention snapped back to Melissa when she rolled in her sleep. Her cover came down exposing the V-line in the dark grey sweater she wore. Firmin licked his lips as he traced the path his knife should take across her throat with his eyes.

The thought sent warm shivers of pleasure through him. He scanned the barn looking for Sean and Elizabeth. They were huddled together in the rear of the building in the corner. It appeared they were sleeping. He glanced at the ceiling above him. Ethan and James had been up there for a long time.

He stepped around the corner of the stall with knife in hand. He gently pulled the latch and pushed the door open. He slowly crept toward her. He could feel her hot breath on his hand as he knelt down and held the knife close to the side of her throat. He was trembling like a lover in anticipation of the first kiss with a new partner. He took a deep breath and leaned in for the first intimate cut.

Thonk! Something dropped in the loft above him. His knife went back into its sheath as Melissa stirred. He quickly stood and strode to the edge of the stall. Behind him he could hear the woman sit up.

"Firmin?"

He could hear the questioning tone in her voice. Confident that his mask was back in place he casually turned around smiling. She looked at him quizzically for a moment then smiled back. His own widened a little further. The waiting would only enhance the ecstasy that would come when he killed her.

"And through covetousness shall they with feigned words make merchandise of you: whose judgment now of a long time lingereth not, and their damnation slumbereth not."

2 Peter 2:3

10

BRING BACK MY BONNIE TO ME

Nick stared at the town shaking his head. It was spread out, but overall it was a small community. The moon was bright enough to show that most of the buildings were still in decent condition. Matt and Justin were amazed to see that some of the homes on one of the blocks had electricity. Nick wasn't fazed at that one bit, but he couldn't believe the name on the sign post. *Rolla. That's a right fine fuck you in the face from the past.*

The three men slinked down the first ally they came to. It connected to a street near a corner building made of brick. Empty, overturned shelves and counters greeted their inspection from a broken window. A cash register lay on its side. Useless coins and dollars littered the abandoned store.

Matt tapped Justin on the shoulder and whispered, "We'll search here first. It looks like a good place for you to hole up in after we're done."

The chubby man nodded. "I'll try to make it up to the roof.

It'll be easier to keep an eye out from there."

Nick scanned the streets for signs of people. Other than the lights coming from a few blocks over, there was no other visual indication the town was occupied. He listened as best he could, but it was hard to hear anything other than the screeching of the cold wind.

The door to the building was off its hinges. It laid just inside in splinters. The trio carefully tread along the walls keeping as close to the ground as possible. Some of the shelving was hard to maneuver over. Justin's boot caught on the edge of one. The metal shrieked as it was drug briefly across the concrete floor before he could free his foot.

When Justin looked up Matt and Nick were staring open mouthed at him. Matt's eyebrows furrowed together as he shook his head. Nick's initial shock from the sudden abrasive noise was quickly replaced by a short laugh when he saw Justin's face.

"Knock it off!" Matt's harsh whisper echoed more loudly in the room than he expected, "This place has been picked clean. Nick, you and me will head on to the houses and see what we can grab. Justin... Stay here and for fucks sake be quiet!"

"Okay. I'll find the stairs to the roof."

"No! Just... stay down here. Please. Man, just hunker low and don't do anything."

Justin bit back the harsh words that flooded into his mind and choked them down. He knew Matt was right. He should have just stayed in the barn with everyone else. He wanted to do something to contribute; more than that he needed to feel useful again. He had only slowed his friends down since their camp at Clyde's had been attacked.

"I'm sorry. For all of this. I won't leave this room."

Matt's features softened. "I don't mean to sound like a dick. There's just so much that can go wrong. You understand, right?"

"Of course I do. I don't want anyone to get hurt because of me."

Nick cleared his throat. "Not to intrude on this tender moment or anything, but we 'ave to get movin' while we still have time to make it back. I don't want the sun showing our pretty faces to whoever fuckin' lives here."

Justin smiled at the Englishmen. It was odd to see all of his hair tucked up into a hat and covered with a hoody. He looked so painfully dull. "Keep him out of trouble."

Nick chuckled much more quietly this time. "He'll be the one babysittin' me."

This was the fourth house they had been through. The others had yielded two heavy blankets and a sleeping bag they could use. This one had been especially promising so far, after finding a partially stocked pantry of food in the basement along with two four-gallon containers of water.

Nick grunted as he lifted one of the thick plastic tubs into Matt's backpack. "This jug must weigh fifteen kilograms."

Matt closed the zipper on the backpack. "I was never good at conversions. I know a gallon of water weighs close to eight and a quarter pounds, so each of these things nets about thirty-three pounds."

Nick smiled. "So I was close. Cut your pounds in half and make a ten bob bit."

Matt hefted his backpack in place as he stood. "What?"

The rocker shook his head. "I can't wait to get back across the pond where people speak proper English."

The men took a few steps toward the stairs. They both froze when the front door opened with a loud creak. Footsteps from above echoed through the basement. They could hear muffled voices, but couldn't make out the conversation.

Matt cursed under his breath. He scanned the space looking for a place for them to hide. He pointed behind the furnace and nodded at Nick. The Englishman quietly slid his backpack off and carefully slid behind the appliance. Matt slipped into the corner next to the stairs. He pulled one of the blankets from his satchel over himself leaving a slit to peer out of.

The footsteps grew louder until they stopped at the top of the stairs. The door handle jiggled as it was turned. More creaking cascaded against their ears as the door was opened. A soft glow flooded the area. From his vantage point Matt watched as a young blonde woman in faded jeans with lantern in hand trudged down the stairs. He held his breath when she opened the pantry door.

She set her lantern down on a small workbench. Stretching she reached for the top shelf and moved some cans around. She reached into the next shelf and did the same thing. Her face scrunched up in a scowl.

"God damn it, Fred. Did you move shit around?" she yelled.

"I haven't touched anything!" A man hollered back.

"Yeah, sure you haven't you fucking prick," she mumbled. The woman pulled a cigarette out of a pack from her shirt pocket and lit it. She took a deep drag and slowly exhaled the smoke. She let it hang in her mouth as she moved more cans around.

"What's taking so long?" The man's voice sounded harsh.

"I can't find any spaghetti rings!"

"Then grab something else. If we're late for this Brother Abel will skin us alive!"

"Fine!" She pulled a few random cans out of the pantry then slammed the door. She grabbed the lantern and headed up the stairs with cigarette still hanging from her mouth.

Matt and Nick barely breathed until they heard the front door slam again. Nick's heart was racing. Cold sweat had beaded up on his brow. His hand was still clutching the handle of the knife he wore at his side.

Matt led the way up the stairs. When they entered the ground floor he grabbed Nick and pulled him down into a squatting position. The street outside the house was filling up with people. Some carried lanterns while others utilized flashlights to find their way in the dark. The mob was heading toward the center of the town to where the block with electricity was located.

Nick breathed heavily while watching them pass. All of those outside were carrying some kind of food or drinks. They didn't make a lot of noise. No conversations were being had. No one laughed or joked with their counterparts. The absence of children among them sent a chill down his spine colder than the wind.

How many of them lost a child or a friend to this? Fuck, how many had to brain their own offspring? The thoughts caused a wave of sympathy to leak from his heart. A part of him wanted to join them; to walk outside and introduce himself. This wasn't the same world anymore though. He knew most groups would force them away at the very least. At worst, well... Americans were never really known for their pacifism.

The glow from their lights slowly faded away as the group moved on. Matt crept to the door and opened it. Nick followed closely. The former Marine jogged to a house across the street and looked around the corner in the direction the mob had gone.

"What ya' thinkin'?" Nick whispered.

"It looks like some kind of town meeting. It may be worth checking out. Thoughts?"

Nick shrugged. "Couldn't hurt to see which way the winds blowin' I reckon."

Matt nodded. He continued to stare around the corner. "Let's give them a bit. They're about forty yards away."

"Bless fuckin' Christ I know what a yard is."

Both men smiled and stifled laughter. Matt finally nodded and shrugged off his backpack. He motioned for Nick to do the same. Without the extra weight the former Marine knew they had a much higher chance of being stealthy. They placed the satchels that held the stolen food and blankets next to the backpacks.

"If we get separated for any reason make sure you check on Justin before heading back to the others. Drag his ass along if you have to, but don't let him wait for me."

Nick nodded. He understood the fierce loyalty the chubby man had to Matt. It wouldn't be easy to convince him to turn tail and run. It was the same he had toward Ethan. Nick knew that he would do everything in his power to keep the lanky giant safe even if it meant taking a bite for him.

At Matt's signal the pair moved out. They ran from house to house as quietly as they could following the glow of lights. The group stopped at an intersection where a crude wooden stage had been constructed. A large fire lit the area with a warm glow.

Nick and Matt crouched next to an ill-kept house with a porch that wrapped around the structure. The Englishman noticed some of the boards were rotten. He gently pulled on one and it silently came away. He nudged Matt. His companion nodded and together they pulled more out of the way. Once an opening was created large enough for them to fit through they crawled under the porch and out of sight.

The bonfire was steadily fed fresh wood as the crowd gathered in front of the makeshift stage. Susan stood on one side of the crudely built structure gazing out over the gathered crowd. Her long, blonde hair was pulled tightly in a ponytail. It flowed midway down the back of the blue, tight-fitting dress she wore. Her sister stood opposite her and was dressed in a similar gown, but her larger breasts filled it out more.

Susan unconsciously crossed her arms in front of her chest. Her sister's perfect breasts were just one of the reasons she was jealous of her. She also hated that her eyes were a darker blue and how Martha always looked amazing in anything she wore. All the men in town wanted her sister, even Scott.

She spotted him easily in the crowd. The clothes he wore, black jeans with a red sweater, framed his toned body. His dark, brown hair was neatly trimmed. His smile was bright white as she followed his gaze to her sister.

Susan's face grew hot despite the autumn wind that was blowing through town. A stabbing ache slammed into her chest almost knocking the breath from her lungs. A wave of jealousy flooded her when she saw Martha returning Scott's smile. She set her jaw and snapped her head forward. She had hoped the rumors of her sister fucking him had been lies, but the shared smile seemed much more than just a friendly gesture. She stared blankly at the crowd and quickly blinked away tears before they could fully form.

Thwang! Thwang! Thwang! The crowd quieted its murmurings as a lone bell tolled. Cold wind screeched between buildings drowning out the crackling of the fire. A loud and steady *clop* echoed from down the street. Heads turned to see

Brother Abel pushing a covered wheelbarrow toward them. His tall frame was unbent by the load in the cart. His face held a wide smile as he nodded to the people he passed.

He pushed the wheelbarrow up the ramp at the rear of the stage. He wiped his hands together a few times and blew into them for warmth. He straightened the black cassock he wore and looked out over the crowd. He motioned at two men close to the fire to add more wood. They scampered to do as commanded.

The preacher raised his hands toward the sky and lifted his head. The group immediately mimicked his actions. They held the pose silently for several minutes until Brother Abel lowered his arms. He motioned for wood to again be placed on the raging bonfire; even though those closest to it were sweating from the heat.

He shivered a bit and blew into his hands again. "Brothers and sisters I've had 'nough of this noisy wind."

Uneasy laughter drifted up from the mob. Brother Abel smiled broadly then his face grew stern. He held his right hand toward the group, palm open. "Let it end."

"Let it end." They echoed as one by one they raised their hands.

The wind slowed. Its eerie cry slacking off until the breeze stopped entirely.

"I'm tired 'ah this cold. Let it end."

Again those gathered repeated him. "Let it end."

The heat of the fire intensified to a painful level for a moment and then the flames died down. Soon a comfortable warmth was radiating out among the flock. People removed their jackets and coats as summerlike temperatures appeared.

Brother Abel smiled as each of his commands was heard and complied with by the elements. The voices promised him they could do miracles. The voices promised that with them at his side he would be a leader in this new world. The voices also whispered to him the price of failure or betrayal.

The twisted holy man licked his lips. He reached out and pulled back the cover from the wheelbarrow. A gasp rose from the crowd as he tipped the cart over and Tom's naked body flopped out on stage. The corpse's stomach was ripped open leaving a full view of its interior workings. Intestines spilled onto the platform as Brother Abel bent over and hoisted the corpse in front of him easily with one hand by the back of its neck.

He shook the body violently. "What was he?"

"Adulterer! Adulterer! Adulterer!" The crowd slowly chanted.

"Who witnessed his suffering?"

"We did! We did! We did!" They yelled.

"How did he die?"

"Screaming! Screaming! Screaming!"

"Sister Susan and Sister Martha were the ones that delivered him 'ta us. Show 'em our gratitude!"

Wild cheering erupted. Each member of the town was doing their best to be louder than their neighbor. Brother Abel let the screams continue for quite a few seconds before raising his arms. Silence immediately fell over the group.

Brother Abel grabbed Tom's leg with his free hand and lifted him into the air. No strain was evident in his features as he casually tossed the body on top of the bonfire. Wood spilled out making way for the corpse to be engulfed by the blaze.

The sickly sweet stench of burnt hair wafted through the air. It was quickly followed by the aroma of steak frying. The pleasant smell lasted only a few moments before morphing into the acrid odor of charred meat. This scent soon combined with boiling bodily fluids to create a noxious cloud of steam that permeated the area.

Many in the crowd gagged. A few couldn't control their reaction and vomited. Three women and one man were openly weeping. Susan and Martha stood rigid and still. Brother Abel closed his eyes and took several deep breaths through his nose. He relished the bouquet the macabre tinder was releasing.

His eyes flew open as a thought came to him. "I'm gonna' give each of these girls 'ah grace 'fer their service to the powers. Sister Susan, 'ya first spotted the sinner in our town. What can the powers grace 'ya with 'fer 'yer loyal work?"

Susan sucked in a sharp breath. She had never seen or heard Brother Abel ask what kind of reward someone might like. She stared at him, mind racing. She tore her gaze away for a moment and pointed toward the crowd. "Scott. I want Scott."

The group stood stunned. Scott's wide eyes darted between Martha, Susan, and Brother Abel. Martha gaped at her sister while a low indecipherable moan escaped her mouth. The twisted pastor's eyebrows raised then settled back down on his smiling face.

"Well, well, well. That's easy 'nuf," Brother Abel laughed. "Scott, 'ya better be findin' a ring 'fer 'yer lady's hand. I now pronounce 'ya man and wife."

Scott took a few steps back and looked around. His friends and neighbors were carefully avoiding eye contact with him. He took a deep breath and looked up at the pastor. "Uh. Brother Abel. Uh. I don't really know her and... Uh. To be honest Martha and I are kinda' together."

Brother Abel's eyes narrowed at Scott's proclamation. The smile fled from his face and was quickly replaced by a snarl. He raised his right hand toward the crowd, palm facing out. The wind returned screeching with unchained fury. Flames leapt upwards toward the heavens from the bonfire's renewed blaze. The crowd rushed to put coats and jackets back on as the temperature dropped rapidly.

"'Ya BELONG 'ta this lady now!" Brother Abel's voice rose to a high pitch as he screamed and pointed at Susan. "The powers command it! The SAME powers that keep the beasts away! Do 'ya wanna' go against their will? Do 'ya wanna make 'em ANGRY!"

The warped holy man clenched his outstretched hand into a fist. The roaring fire died away to embers. The half-melted and charred corpse of the intruder continued to hiss and pop. The wind wailed a few more seconds then silence fell among the gathering. Brother Abel crossed his arms over his chest and smiled down at Scott. "Well?"

The young man stood shaking. He looked hopelessly at Martha. His shoulders slumped in defeat. "As the powers will it, Brother Abel."

Susan smiled at her sister. Martha turned her head away from the smug look. She fought for control against the rising tide of anger and hurt that wanted her to attack her sister. Scott had been her lover for the last three months in secret. They had been making plans to escape the crazed man and head to Arizona where his mother was living. Part of the plan was to take her sister with them.

Martha looked at Scott. He was being congratulated on his 'marriage' by people in the crowd. He looked dazed as he shook hands. She gritted her teeth in frustration. There was no way to know if they could still pull off their plan, but it was certain that they would have to leave her sister behind now.

Brother Abel's voice snapped her attention back to him. "Sister Martha, 'yah stopped him from stealin' from 'yer brethren. What can the powers grace 'ya with 'fer 'yer loyal work?"

Martha grimaced from the memory. She had tackled the man to keep him from running off with *her* ration of food for the month. She didn't feel like a community hero at all. In fact she felt very selfish at the moment. Martha glared at her sister before turning to the pastor. "I don't want my sister to have Scott."

Whispered conversations sprang up as the crowd processed her request. Brother Abel raised his hands. Silence fell. He studied Martha's face for a moment. He then looked at the scowl on Susan's. He bit his tongue in thought and nodded to himself before breaking out into another smile.

"Why don't 'ya come on up here while we figure this out," he motioned to Scott. "This is vexin' isn't it folks?"

People in the crowd nodded their heads at the pastor's question. Scott climbed the stairs on the side closest to Martha. She rushed into his arms. They hugged each other for a second and he pulled her face towards him for a gentle kiss before he softly pushed her away to stand next to Brother Abel.

"Ya'll know the voices guide me. They give me insight in 'ta how best 'ta guide my flock."

"We do Brother Abel!" Voices called out.

The preacher patted Scott on the back a few times. "Well, just a moment ago I asked 'em to give me 'ah sign. I asked 'em to show me where Scott belongs."

With lightning speed the pastor's right hand drew a knife from somewhere in his cassock. In the same fluid movement he buried the blade deep into the back of Scott's head. The tip of the weapon appeared through the skin just above his left eye. A small trickle of blood seeped from the wound. Scott's body straightened and became rigid. He did not fall.

"He belongs in the ground! The voices said I'd get 'ah sign. When he kissed Martha he committed 'ah grave sin. Married man kissin' another woman! Adulterer!"

The crowd looked on in shock. Susan and Martha both wailed and lunged for Scott. With his left arm Brother Abel shoved Susan off the stage before she could get close to him.. With his right hand he clutched Martha painfully by the shoulder when she got within reach. The force of his grip brought her to her knees. Scott swayed on unsteady legs.

Brother Abel bent over, pulling Martha close to him. "Ya' know what happens to harlots. Ya' didn't want him to kiss ya', did ya'? Ya' didn't wanna' be kissed by yer' sister's husband? Right?"

She nodded her head rapidly up and down. The twisted man pushed her to the ground. Grabbing the handle of the knife he flicked his wrist twisting the sharp steel embedded in Scott's skull. Limbs flailed as the doomed man's brain sent a few final signals through his spine. Brother Abel placed his left hand on the back of the dead man's head and held it steady as he pulled his knife out. Scott toppled face-first off the stage and landed with a *thud*.

The preacher's eyes were wide. Froth formed at the corners of his mouth. He grabbed Martha by her ponytail and yanked her to her feet. He held the bloody knife in front of her face. "Marriage is 'til death do ya' part. I already pronounced 'em man and wife. This was the only way! The voices told me this was the only way to fulfill the grace I promised 'yah!"

She was shaking. She felt cold all over when she stared him in the eyes. Gradually his face softened and he let go of her hair. He wiped his lips with the back of his sleeve. He tucked the gory weapon away in his cassock.

A low moan from the edge of the stage caught their attention. Susan was hugging a still twitching Scott. She rocked back and forth on her knees as tears fell from her face. Martha furiously wiped away at her own fearing that Brother Abel would kill her if she showed any compassion for her dead lover.

A gentle touch from him made her cringe. The preacher's face had lines of worry etched on it. "Go to her. It's 'yer sisterly duty to take care of her durin' her time 'ah grief. Her husband just died after all."

Martha blinked vacantly. "You're fucking crazy."

Brother Abel winced. Anger replaced the compassion on his face. He slapped her with the back of his hand sending her reeling dangerously close to the edge of the stage. "I'm blessed with the light 'ah truth 'yah ignorant bitch. If it wasn't 'fer me this whole fuckin' place would—"

"Brother Abel! Brother Abel!"

Shouts rang out from down the street where a small group of four men and two women was approaching. They were dragging something along behind them on a plastic sled. Her head was ringing from the blow, but as they got closer Martha could make out the shape of a man on the sled. He had a large belly and was bound hand to foot.

A tall, broad-shouldered man stepped in front of them when they got close to the stage. Like the others closest to him, he had a rifle slung over his shoulder. "We found this stranger hiding at the old Corner Quick Stop."

Brother Abel jumped off the stage and landed lightly on his feet. He knelt down next to the restrained man and gently stroked his face. "It looks like ya' got the sin of gluttony on 'yer soul, brother. Don't worry. We'll be takin' care of that soon enough."

"Anyone who is found will be thrust through, and anyone who is captured will fall by the sword. Their little ones also will be dashed to pieces before their eyes; their houses will be plundered and their wives ravished. Behold, I am going to stir up the Medes against them, who will not value silver or take pleasure in gold. And their bows will mow down the young men, they will not even have compassion on the fruit of the womb, nor will their eye pity children."

Isaiah 13:15 -18

WE THREE KINGS

After returning with their stolen goods Nick hastily explained what they had witnessed. Matt silently held on to Melissa as the Englishmen weaved the tale of their encounter. Firmin paced back and forth shaking his head obviously frustrated at the language barrier. Nick's eyes never left Ethan's when he got to the part about Justin being captured.

"No one else dies!"

Nick clenched his jaw. Matt wasn't happy about leaving Justin either, but he was practical enough to understand they couldn't take on an entire town. "Did you not fucking hear what I said? Their leader is some kind of witch. A fucking barmy, off his fucking rocker, witch!"

Ethan crossed his arms over his chest and glared at Nick, Melissa, and Matt. "I heard it. I'm telling you we need to go get him out of there!"

"I'm with Ethan!" James grunted.

"So am I!" Sean and Elizabeth echoed.

Nick looked to the other adults for help. He knew that Ethan and the kids would be a problem, but he had no clue on how to dissuade them.

Matt cleared his throat. "I was there. I saw what happened. We might be able to take a few of them down with us, but down we'd go. Justin wouldn't want any of us to get hurt trying to save him. Especially you kids."

James frantically shook his head. "We're not kids anymore. We're survivors just like you."

"Justin would come for us. Any of us!" Elizabeth declared.

"We have to do something!" Sean insisted.

"We *are* going to do something!" Matt roared. "We're getting the hell out of here and as far away from these nut bags as fast as we can. End of discussion. Gather your shit!"

"But—"

"No fucking 'buts' about it, James. He's already dead and unless you want us to join him get your shit. All of you. We're heading out in five!"

Tears instantly fell from Elizabeth at Matt's harsh command. She sprinted for the loft. Sean glared at the former Marine before taking off after her.

"This is fucked up," James mumbled as he walked away.

Firmin shrugged. He looked around at the other adults and then followed the children up the ladder into the loft.

"You're seriously going to just leave him?" Ethan fumed.

"You didn't see what we did. We don't have time for a wobbler, mate. We need to leg it before those bloody people realize we're here."

Matt's eyes narrowed. He pushed past Nick and jabbed a finger in Ethan's chest. "He's my best friend. I've known him my entire life. Don't you see this is killing me!"

"All I see is someone who doesn't give a shit about saving his friends!"

Nick interwove himself between the two men and shoved them apart.

"Enough!" Melissa screamed. "We can't do this. Not here. Not now. We have to figure out what to do."

The barn grew quiet. Ethan glared at Matt. The former Marine wanted nothing more than to vent his frustrations of the situation through violence. He knew Ethan was only thinking of Justin's wellbeing, but it was hard not to lash out.

Matt took a deep breath and opened his mouth to speak. Melissa grabbed him by the arm. "Stop! Listen."

Everyone held their breath. Not a sound came from anywhere.

"God Damn it!" Matt bolted for the loft with Nick in tow.

A hasty search of the upper barn yielded no kids or a Firmin. Their backpacks and weapons were gone as well. The upstairs ladder had been moved. Glancing outside Nick grunted. They must have silently climbed out during the argument downstairs.

Matt stood at the ledge of the loft and looked down on the worried faces of Melissa and the lanky giant. "Grab your guns. Ethan, it looks like you get your wish. Those fucking kids ran off to try to save Justin."

Elizabeth held on to Sean's hand as they ran. James outdistanced the pair by a few hundred feet. The semi-automatic rifle swaying in his arms as his legs carried him closer to their captured friend. They ran as swiftly as they could through the darkness hoping they weren't already too late.

Like a shepherd keeping a watchful eye on his flock Firmin loped along behind the children just out of their sight. He wasn't entirely sure what was happening, but he knew that it involved Justin in some way. He liked the plump man with the gentle eyes. Besides he wasn't going to let the kids run off by themselves.

He was thankful to be out of the barn and away from the dark impulses that had crawled like worms into his brain. Even now he could feel the urges resting just on the edge of his consciousness. He fought down images of Melissa's head in his arms as he ran. He could feel anticipation continuing to creep along his skin at the thought.

He snapped his mind back from the thoughts and concentrated on putting one foot in front of the other. He could clearly see Sean and Elizabeth now and could make out James' moving form in the dark ahead of them. Firmin ran from his familiar demons towards a whole new world of them.

Dim lighting revealed the walls inside of the building were covered in a pirate theme. Black tapestries with a white skull and two crossed cutlass's adorned the hallways. Justin was only vaguely aware of the surroundings. His heart pounded in his chest as he was roughly pulled by his captors. He dimly noticed walls lined with lockers and several open doors while he marched along.

His ragged breathing and echoing footsteps of the crowd were the only sounds he heard. No one spoke, not even in a whisper to their neighbor. The only relief he felt was that Brother Abel had moved ahead of the group and was out of his line of sight. The man made his stomach clench in knots. Something evil was hiding behind his smiles and laughter.

The group slowed when they came to a set of double doors. Justin thought he saw light streaming out from underneath. His initial thought was verified when the doors were flung open to reveal a lit staircase leading down.

A tall well-built man with brown hair stepped in front of his other three captors. "Brother Abel told me to come down alone with this fucker. The rest of you close up and wait for me here. Come on fat-ass." The burly man grabbed the shackles on his hands and pulled him.

Justin wobbled a bit as he was led down the stairs. He heard the doors close behind him after he took a few steps. The temperature got warmer and he smelled sulfur as he descended into the basement of the school. He heard a low humming sound that he couldn't place. When they reached the bottom of the stairs a cold chill crept over him as he spotted Brother Abel.

He sat behind a wide, wooden oak table in a plush looking leather chair. Next to him was a large steel trunk with a lock on it. Other than a teakettle and three small cups the table was empty. Tall, dark curtains were closed behind him concealing the rest of the basement. He smiled and pointed across the desk to a chair that mirrored the one he sat in. Justin's escort shoved him down onto it. The large man then stood behind Brother Abel and crossed his arms.

The smiling holy man poured three cups of hot tea from the kettle. He slid one across to Justin and held another up to the man next to him. "Here 'ya go, Keith. Sugar already added."

"Thank you, Brother Abel." The man took the offered cup and sipped it.

Justin studied the man seated across from him. The smile on his face seemed genuine, but there was a dangerous glint in his eyes. It hinted at a touch of madness. The former pastor picked up his cup and held the warm container between chilled hands. He inhaled the steam as it rose never taking his eyes away from the smiling man.

Keith glared at Justin. "Say 'thank you' before I rip your balls off!"

"Now, now… we don't need 'ta be rude to our guest," Brother Abel absently waved a hand at the large man. "You'll have 'ta forgive him. He ain't as cultured as we are."

"Thank… Thank you, sir."

Keith slowly nodded his approval of Justin's gratitude, but the glare never left the man's dark brown eyes. He took another drink. The small cup looked comical in his large, meaty hands.

Brother Abel leaned forward in his chair. "Go ahead and warm 'yer belly. I gathered all the herbs 'fer it and blended it myself. Tell me what 'ya think."

The fallen pastor took a sip. It was sweet at first, but contained a slightly alcoholically bitter and salty aftertaste. It took him a few seconds to place the flavors. "Anise, mint, and chamomile?"

A wide smile splayed across Brother Abel's face. "Yes and 'ah shot of rum! 'Ah course a few other secret ingredients, but 'ya know 'yer plants."

"Gardening was a hobby of mine. I had a… friend that was enthusiastic about it."

"Ya' can call me Brother Abel. What's 'yer name, stranger?"

"Justin. Justin Grady."

"What was 'yer callin' before God's judgement cleansed

the world?"

Justin winced at the question. His interrogator caught the movement and nodded gravely at him. He stared into his cup a few seconds then mumbled, "I wasn't anything. A drunk on my worst days, a mental train wreck on my best."

Keith stifled a yawn with his hand. The large man downed the rest of his tea and gently set the cup back on the table before stretching.

Brother Abel glanced over his shoulder. "Sounds like 'yer a bit tuckered out. Grab a seat and relax. 'Ya been workin' so hard lately, Keith. 'Ya deserve a break."

"Thank you, Brother Abel." The bodyguard pulled a smaller chair to the table and slumped down in it.

Turning his attention back to Justin he smiled. "Brother, it sure sounds like 'ya let 'yer life go to shit. Life is the greatest gift 'ah God and you were just pissin' it away."

The chubby man continued to stare into his cup while the holy man leaned back in his seat and regarded his prisoner. "We need 'ta figure out what 'ta do with you."

Justin felt the blood drain from his face. He nervously sipped at his tea while the man across the desk stared at him. Silence fell on the room for several minutes. He dropped the cup when a loud *SNORT* erupted from Keith. The fragile porcelain shattered when it hit the cold concrete of the basement floor. The large man had fallen asleep.

Brother Abel slowly stood. His eyes narrowed slightly as the smile on his face took on a malevolent appearance. He reached out and gently shook the larger man. When there was no response he bent over, lifted the man's chin, and forced his left eyelid wide. Drool fell from his lips as his mouth lolled open.

Brother Abel straightened and rubbed his hands together. "I like this man. I really do. He was such a dedicated member of the flock."

His voice sounded like it was echoing down a long hallway. Justin's fear vanished as he felt a deep relaxation flow over his body. He blinked several times as his eyes became blurry. He looked at the still steaming and untouched cup that had been in front of Brother Abel. He pushed himself up from the chair, but didn't have the strength to run. Justin only barely made it to his feet before toppling over.

Brother Abel, still smiling, easily lifted him and laid him on the table. He pulled a set of keys from his pocket and unlocked the chest. He carefully removed shackles and chains and placed them on the table next to the unconscious prisoner. Returning to the chest he retrieved a black bag and set it next to Justin's head.

He pulled the chubby man's shirt off and tossed it on the floor. He looped the chains under the table and clamped the restraints to his victim's wrists and ankles. He hummed while walking around the table examining his work. After making a few adjustments the shackles barely twitched when pressure was applied to them.

Still humming, he drug a folding table from behind his chair. He set it up next to the wooden one. He picked up Keith and casually slung him across it. The well-muscled man continued to snore loudly.

Brother Abel opened his bag and rummaged through it. He smiled broadly as he pulled out a hammer and ice pick. He walked back to Keith and stood silently next to him for a few seconds. He gently patted the large man's head as if he was a dog.

The holy man sadly shook his head as tears formed in his eyes. "Keith, I'm real sorry for this. It's 'yer fault I gotta' do this 'ya know! 'Yer tryin' to stir folks up. Tryin' to raise them up against me. I can't have that!"

Brother Abel held Keith's left eye opened while positioning the ice pick just under the top lid. When he was satisfied he grabbed the hammer and with one quick, powerful tap inserted the hardened steel into his brain. The snoring stopped for a brief moment while his patient's right foot twitched a few times.

He breathed a sigh of relief when a trickle of blood flowed from the eye socket and the snoring resumed. He walked over and pulled back the curtain. Rows and rows of shelves and tables filled the basement alongside hospital equipment. Every one of them contained several aquariums filled with blood. At least one oxygenator was placed in each causing frothy red bubbles to coat the surface. He stopped briefly in front of one of the tanks to dip his hand in and adjust the nozzle on one of the small devices. The smell of sulfur permeated the area. He wiped his bloody hand on his cassock while smiling at a sleeping and helpless Keith.

A bright light pounded excruciatingly into his brain. He clamped his eyes shut, but they were forced open again for a few seconds by unkind fingers. The light vanished with a *click*. He blinked groggily a few times trying to rid himself of the effects from the glare before closing his eyes. A voice murmured above him, but he couldn't make out what was being said.

His drug addled brain had trouble comprehending what was going on. He knew that Matt and Nick were heading into town. He thought he might be able to talk Matt into taking him along. He didn't feel well enough to go anywhere. His head hurt. He felt sweat running off his face. His stomach was queasy.

He licked his dry lips. "Go without me. I'm sick. Matt, I'm sick. I don't know what's wrong."

A pillow was placed under his head. A rag tenderly dabbed across his forehead. He felt a cup being placed on his lips. He gulped down the water as soon as it hit his mouth. It was cool and refreshing. His stomach cramps eased a bit when the liquid settled in it.

"Wakey, wakey, eggs, and bakey."

The voice sounded familiar, but he couldn't place it. The sound unsettled him. A small part of his brain screamed at him to run. He didn't understand where the sudden feeling of dread was coming from. He forced his eyes open. A blurry, smiling face filled his vision. The smile…

Fear brought adrenaline coursing through his veins. Memories of hiding in an old convenience store came back to him along with the wonderful experience of being drug out of the building at gunpoint by a small group of townsfolk.

He looked around groggily. He couldn't move his arms or

legs and it took him a moment to realize he had been restrained. Next to him was a table concealing something underneath a blanket. He smelled blood. He thought he heard a low ragged breathing sound.

"Come on, Justin. Time's 'ah waistin'. I want 'ya 'ta see somethin' before we move on 'ta 'yer particular sins."

More wakeful now he focused his gaze on Brother Abel. "What did you do to me?"

"Besides the GHB? Nothin'. Not a dang thing. Not yet."

"GHB?"

"Gamma-hydroxybutyrate. In the simplest terms it's 'ah metabolite that's 'ah depressant to the central nervous system. That means it functions as 'ah relaxant. The body makes it naturally. 'Ah course 'ya can also synthesize it 'yerself if 'ya know what 'yer doin'. I happen to know what I'm 'ah doin'."

Justin's mind continued to clear as he listened to Brother Abel speak. "Who are you?"

The older man glanced up at the ceiling of the basement then grimly looked down at him. "In the old world I was a doctor. I was a neurosurgeon to be more precise."

The bound man noticed the change in his captor's voice. Each syllable was pronounced cleanly and effortlessly.

"I worked at Kansas Spine and Specialty Hospital in Wichita. I was… let go a few months before the virus spread."

"Virus? What virus?" Justin's words came out barely above a whisper.

"The virus that caused all of this," he spread his arms wide. "I started hearing voices over a year ago. At first I thought I was going crazy. Who wouldn't? But then… things they told me started coming true."

"A virus made you hear voices?"

"What? No! How absurd," Brother Abel laughed. "The voices were otherworldly forces, obviously. They started whispering to me in my dreams. They warned me that the virus was coming."

"You think a virus knocked everyone out, and then woke them up as monsters?"

"No. The Rapture happened, and THEN the virus turned everyone into monsters. That's what the voices told me."

Looking up into the calm visage of the man standing next to him raised doubt to the state of his sanity. "So… It's a virus? Not demonic possession?"

"You don't sound convinced."

"I'm not. God took his faithful home and the armies of Hell now walk among us."

Anger flashed across Brother Abel's face. "Agree to disagree."

"That doesn't even make any sense. How can a virus turn people into super-strong cannibals? They heal faster than any—"

A fist slammed into the left side of his jaw silencing him. A sharp *crack* resounded through the basement as Justin's head rocked from the force of the blow. The lower part of his face felt numb for a second and then exploded into agony when he tried to close his mouth.

"I said 'agree to disagree' you worthless tub of shit!"

Tears streamed down his face as he fought against the urge to scream. He tried to focus on Brother Abel's face, but his vision was clouded over. Try as he might he couldn't repress a low moan from escaping.

"Damn it," Brother Abel bent over him and lightly turned his head to examine his jaw. "Well, the good news is I think it's only dislocated. Sometimes I forget how strong I am now. Try to relax while I set it. If you bite me I'll gut you like a hog."

He placed his hands on each side of Justin's jaw. He put his thumbs in the injured man's mouth and rested them on his lower back molars. He slowly and firmly pushed down and back. Justin's eyes squinted in pain as his jaw popped into place.

"There you go. It will be sore for a few weeks but then it—"

Brother Abel stopped talking. He began chuckling. "I'm sorry about that. Old habits die hard. You won't have to put up with the pain for too much longer."

Justin blinked away the rest of his tears. "What does that mean?"

The old man's face lit up with a smile. "I'm glad you asked. See, when the voices started telling me what was coming I prepared. I moved to this little town about a week before it all started. I got all my equipment ready just like I was told to."

Justin stared at Brother Abel. A cold numbness was slowly drifting over him. Questions spun through his head like a spider's web. Each thought splintering into more questions with every imagined answer that was not forthcoming.

"I stored all of it until the Rapture came. Then I quietly set up down here," Brother Abel pulled back the curtain. "As you can see I have been very busy."

Justin gaped at the rows of tanks. The acrid odor of sulfur became more prevalent as they bubbled and foamed. Machines of various sizes and unknown purposes to him hummed away as they went about their work.

"What... What's in the tanks?"

"Your future."

He walked past the first two rows and stopped in front of a large, one-hundred gallon floor tank. He plucked a net from the wall and dug around in the tank with it. When he felt weight catch he pulled it up. Staring back at him from the net was a severed head twice the size of a normal man's. It was greyish like the smaller creepers, but had a jutting forehead and coal black eyes. Its oversized and sharpened teeth were desperately trying to chew through the nylon netting.

Tubes were inserted into the left and right carotid arteries on the monster's neck. Blood was pumped into the head by the tubes via one of the two oxygenators in the tank. Brother Abel rubbed the creature's hair affectionately then dropped it back in the bloody tank.

Justin froze. He was transfixed and couldn't look away from the tank. Every few seconds the head would bump against the glass. Its lips were open in a silent scream as it peered into the outside world.

His eyes started darting from tank to tank. In one he saw a severed arm scuttling along the bottom. In another he saw a hand gripping a foot tightly. He finally tore his gaze away when he witnessed a group of eyeballs swimming around in one of the larger tanks like a school of fish.

He dazedly stared at the ceiling. Brother Abel was standing over him smiling. The surgeon licked his top lip as he stared down at him. "What do you think of my work?"

"Why are they still moving? They're not whole... Why are they still moving?" Justin's mouth dully intoned the thoughts in his head.

"Because the virus is a medical marvel! As long as the organs and limbs have oxygenated blood they can survive. The virus provides a level of cellular regeneration completely unheard of in modern medicine. It can affect each host organism in a different way right down to how long it takes for the virus to infect it."

The bound man took in every word the twisted doctor was saying. Looking at the gory contents of the tanks it was hard to find an argument to refute the proof at hand. Except that Brother Abel also acknowledged that the Rapture did happen. Which meant that God was directly involved in all of this. So if God had a hand in this then so did the devil.

"Another fascinating aspect of the infected tissue is its ability for self-preservation under the most extreme circumstances," Brother Abel babbled excitedly. "The best example I can think of is to show you what I've done to Keith."

The holy man pulled back the cover on the other table with the enthusiasm of a child on Christmas morning. Beaming with pride he pointed at the still unconscious body lying next to Justin. A shudder ran through the chubby man. He couldn't stop the scream from escaping his throat as he stared at the horror across from him.

Staring at him was a second head perched on Keith's neck and shoulder. It blinked at him with hate-filled eyes. Its mouth opened and closed exposing wickedly jagged teeth. Red marks ran like veins down the shared neck and into Keith's chest.

Ignoring Justin's outburst, Brother Abel calmly continued, "The hardest part was getting one of the veins attached. Once I did that the virus took over. As you can see Keith is still very much alive. Lobotomized, but alive. I expect his transformation will be one of the more interesting ones I have studied."

Small blots of saliva formed at the corners of his mouth as his smile widened. The demented surgeon held up a scalpel. "Now, let's see what we can do about 'yer sin 'ah gluttony, brother."

"Surely, thus says the LORD, "Even the captives of the mighty man will be taken away, and the prey of the tyrant will be rescued; for I will contend with the one who contends with you, and I will save your sons. I will feed your oppressors with their own flesh, and they will become drunk with their own blood as with sweet wine; and all flesh will know that I, the LORD, am your Savior and your Redeemer, the Mighty One of Jacob."

Isaiah 49:25 -26

12

ONE FOR THE DAME

"Okay they're gone."

Sean and Elizabeth breathed a sigh of relief when James verified the small group of townsfolk had passed by them. The kids crawled out from under the old green Chevy truck where they had been hiding. They could hear the tromping of feet echoing back at them from around the corner.

Sean nodded at James and pointed in the direction the group had gone. "That was a lucky break."

"Hell yeah it was," James whispered smiling. "Of course a new guy in town would cause a lot of buzz. Did you understand anything else they were talking about?"

"It sounded bad," Elizabeth's voice was quiet. "Whenever someone says things like 'the holy fire of retribution' it can never be good."

"No kidding," Sean put his 9mm pistol back into its holster. "Why would they take him to the school?"

Elizabeth shrugged. "It sounds like this 'Brother Abel' is big on lessons. What better place to teach than school?"

James shifted on his feet impatiently. "We better hurry

before something happens."

"Yeah," Sean scratched his nose. "How do we find the school?"

"Let's break into a house and grab a phonebook. There should be a map of the town in one along with an address to the school."

Both boys smiled at the young woman. Justin put his hands together a few times in mock applause. "Just look at you. Little miss goody two-shoes has grown up to be a criminal mastermind."

Elizabeth blushed. "Shut up, James. Come on, Sean. We might as well try this house first."

Elizabeth knelt down in the backseat of an old tan Buick. She pulled a stinking, half-moldy blanket over her head to conceal herself from any roaming patrols that might come by. She held her shotgun close to her chest as she kept a watchful eye on the block in front of the school.

Sean and James were bent over the lock on the doors. Dim light from inside the building was barely enough to make out what they were doing. She watched as James worked pieces of wire into the lock and moved them around. He shook the doors after a few moments and then pointed something out to Sean on the ground next to them. Her boyfriend shook his head and motioned at James to give him the tools he carried.

Sean knelt down next to the door. His hands inserted the wires into the lock. He patiently moved them back and forth while James stomped back to the car Elizabeth was hiding in. Flustered, he got into the backseat with her.

"He won't let me smash the fucking glass on the doors."

"That's a stupid idea. If anyone sees broken glass they'll raise a ruckus. That's the last thing we need."

James glared at the girl for a second before looking over at his friend. Sean was still slowly working at the lock. "Yeah, you're both right. When he sets out to do something it's hard to change his mind isn't it?"

Elizabeth smiled. "That's one of the reasons I love him."

"Do you?"

"What's that?"

"Love him?"

She looked at James. "I think I do."

"So how far has he gotten?"

She slapped him playfully on his shoulder. "That's none of your business!"

"I'm just saying if you like him go for it. Or let him go for it," James gave her a cocky smile. "You let me go for it."

"Shut up! I told you not to talk about that!"

Her fury washed over him like a cold wind. James pushed himself against the door. He fumbled for the handle as her eyes burned hatefully into him.

Elizabeth's mouth twitched in rage. "Don't you understand? It's the reason I didn't get to go to Heaven! What we did was wrong in the eyes of God!"

James's fear turned into irritation. "Fuck God. If he's all powerful, fuck him. If he did this to us, fuck him!"

Elizabeth stared at him. Her anger gave way to shock. James didn't let up. "He sent zombies here to kill us. He took away people we cared about. He made us do things to survive. He made me kill—"

James threw open the door. He rolled out of the backseat glaring at her the entire time. "Stay here and keep quiet."

The Z.O.D. sergeant tromped towards the doors of the school. He bent down and grabbed a rock just smaller than his fist. He shoved Sean out of the way. Glass was shattering before the orphan could regain his footing.

James ignored the flash of anger that swept across Sean's face as he looked back at him. "Let's go."

The boys crept along the empty halls of the school. The flickering of emergency lights flickered gave off barely enough of a glow to see by. Both of them thought how crowded the halls must have been at one time. But now, they were grateful for the absence of other people. No matter how hard they tried to walk softly, their footsteps echoed off the walls. Sean put a hand on James's shoulder to stop him. When the older boy turned Sean pointed at his feet. James thought for a moment then grudgingly nodded his head. After the pair removed their shoes they continued roaming the halls.

Their sock covered feet muffled the sounds of their approach, but the chill of the cold concrete floor soon had their feet uncomfortably numb. Teeth chattering, they reluctantly slipped their heavy boots back on. James barely finished tying his when a muted shriek flooded the hallway.

"Justin?" Sean snapped his attention towards the direction the sound came from.

James was off in a flash. The concept of stealth was instantly abandoned at the cry of duress from their friend. Sean followed the other boy without a second thought, pulling his pistol as he ran.

James bolted around a corner. He slid to a halt as he came face to face with three armed men holding rifles. The boy brought his AK-47 up at the same time the strangers leveled their guns at him. He took a few cautious steps backwards.

The oldest of the men took a step toward him. "Stop! Drop it kid! We don't wanna' hurt you! Drop it!"

Sean managed to stop his momentum before clearing the corner into the line of sight of whoever James was aiming at. He held his pistol up at the ready. He watched James, looking for a sign of what he should do next.

"The three of you have my friend. I want him back."

Three. Okay there are three of them. Sean slowly sidestepped until he was resting against the hallway wall. He took a few deep breaths to steady his nerves.

The older man's rifle lowered an inch before he raised it back up. "Your friend was caught spying on us. I'm sorry, kid. I really am. If you put your gun down we'll take you to him. You can talk to our leader. Brother Abel will listen to you."

"Yeah, I heard how reasonable he is," James spat. "Holy fire of retribution, burning people, murder… sounds like a real socialite."

The older man spoke softer. "You don't know what it's been like here, boy. He has powers. He can do things nobody else can. It's real magic."

Sean slinked away from his friend down the hall. If James saw him moving away from the confrontation, he made no show of it. He knew there was an intersection not too far away.

He hoped it led behind the people James was talking with. He fervently wished he could convey his plan to his friend.

"Real magic? Like maybe the Rapture and then a bunch of zombies running around?" James laughed.

"No. He keeps the monsters away. He told us if we follow him he would keep us safe. We laughed at him. We laughed until we saw what he can do!"

James could see light streaming out from under a set of double doors the men stood by. His mind raced for an idea to get by them. He tried his best to sound curious as he said, "What can he do?"

"I've seen him heal people with just a touch of his hand. More than that... the monsters are scared of him! The last time we were attacked Brother Abel came running right out in the middle of them. He yelled at them to leave and they... left. They just stopped what they were doing and ran."

James listened intently as the man spoke. The intensity in his voice left no doubt that the man believed what he was saying. The boy studied the other two. Their body language gave him no clue as to what their intentions were, but he could tell they were scared.

"I'm glad he's keeping you safe, but no matter what he can do it doesn't give him any right to hold my friend prisoner."

The older man's jaw clenched. "The world's changed, kid. This is how things are. Now, set your gun down and put your hands above your head."

James caught a shadow of movement from down the hallway behind the men. He hoped Sean had managed to work his way behind them and that it wasn't another one of their friends.

"What happens if I say no?"

James saw the man's friends share a nervous glance. The older man blinked at him. "If you say no then we have one hell of a problem. I'm getting real tired of having that gun pointed at me! So just put it down before you do something stupid!"

James narrowed his gaze. He focused on the older man. "All I want is my friend back. Just get him. No one has to die."

The man's voice rose. "Boy, if you don't get that gun on the ground in the next ten seconds we're going to light you up!"

James thoughts screamed in frustration. It didn't have to be like this, but if he was going to die he was going to take this asshole with him. His vision became tunneled as more adrenaline pumped into his system. Something moved behind his target, but he was too focused to see what it was.

The older man held his rifle tightly against his shoulder. "I'm serious, kid! Ten, nine, eight, seven, six, five, fo—"

The Frenchmen glided from one patch of darkness to the next as he approached the car the older boy had been in. He could see Elizabeth staring at the school from the backseat. Firmin grimaced as James smashed the glass on the door.

He didn't understand why the kids would split up. It made no sense to him. Of course they were just kids so chances are it was something he could chalk up to youthful inexperience. It was the same kind of inexperience that would lead to him being shot by the young lady if he didn't give her a chance to see him coming.

He switched direction and headed to the side of the school. When he came even with the car he slowly walked toward it with his hands up. Elizabeth flung the door open and motioned at him to join her.

He vigorously shook his head and waved at her to follow him. He marched backwards toward the building the boys had entered keeping his eyes on her. Elizabeth leapt out of the car and ran after him. He smiled when she drew near. He turned his back to her.

Entering the school was easy enough. James had left the door open. Firmin closed it behind them. Anything more than a casual glance would alert someone that the glass was busted, but it was the best he could do to try to keep their activities clandestine.

He pulled his knife from its sheath. He held it up and pointed at the similar blade Elizabeth had at her hip. Taking the hint, the young woman drew her weapon. The pair carefully prowled down the hall. They followed the sounds of footsteps. The steady rhythm suddenly stopped. Firmin waited a minute, but when they did not continue he nudged Elizabeth to keep moving.

They walked for a few minutes and then stopped when they heard a muffled scream. It was hard to tell where exactly the sound came from, but Firmin was confident that he and the girl set off in the general direction. Shortly after the yell faded he heard familiar footsteps echoing away from them much louder and faster.

Elizabeth started to rush past him. He snaked an arm across her shoulder and pulled her back. She stared fearfully into his eyes. He held a finger in front of his lips and shook his head. She relaxed in his grip. Letting her go he walked in front of her.

He heard someone yelling in English. He hastened his steps when he heard James's voice responding. Elizabeth tapped him on his arm. When he looked at her she was holding up three fingers. He didn't understand what she meant, but nodded at her anyway.

The stranger's voice spoke again and was no longer screaming. Firmin hoped it meant that conflict was being avoided. The tone of James's reply shattered that brief feeling. He continued down the hall with the young woman as the conversation went on. A flicker of movement ahead made him raise his knife and hold his breath.

He slowly let it out when he recognized Sean's relieved face rushing toward them from an intersection in the hallway. The boy hugged Elizabeth briefly. Firmin ground his teeth in frustration as the two kids whispered back and forth. Finally Sean turned to him and held up three fingers.

Firmin pointed at himself, then at Sean and Elizabeth. The kids shook their heads and each held up three fingers. Firmin's nod was sincere this time. There were three of them. Three people that needed to be taken care of quietly.

Firmin pointed at his knife. Sean grimly pulled the machete out that he wore on his hip. With Sean leading the way the trio headed past the intersection to another hallway. They followed the sound of conversation back around until they came up behind the group.

All three men were pointing rifles at James. The kid held his

AK-47 up and was aiming at the man he was speaking with. Firmin's face flushed. He slowly stalked toward the group. He wanted to be able to see the man's face when he slit his throat. He licked his lips in anticipation as the distance closed between them.

He vaguely registered Elizabeth and Sean walking with him. A momentary rush of anger slipped over him. He didn't want to share the kills with anyone. Cold practicality overruled his greed. He needed each one of the kids to at least incapacitate one of the other men. He gently nudged Sean towards the man on the right. Elizabeth was shaking, but she veered a little to left understanding Firmin's intentions.

The man's voice rose. Firmin couldn't understand what he was saying until he heard numbers. He knew simple English numbers. The man must have made some ultimatum and was now counting down. Time was running out. He couldn't relax and enjoy this like he wanted to.

With a burst of speed Firmin lashed out. He pulled the man close to him. With one quick move he jerked his victim's head up and slashed with his knife. A spray of blood erupted from the ruined neck and coated James's face as arteries were severed.

The man's vocal cords gurgled as the knife separated flesh. He weakly clutched at his throat in a futile effort to stem the gouts of blood rushing out. Firmin pulled back harder on his head. He looked into the man's eyes as they clouded over in death. The rifle didn't even bark out a single shot before dropping from lifeless hands.

Firmin turned to see Sean and Elizabeth. Both of them held bloody knives in their hands. At their feet lay the bodies of the other two men. One was feebly trying to crawl away. Blood pumped from the gashes in their necks for a few more seconds before trickling off. Both men were finally still.

The girl's knife slipped from her grasp and landed in the fast spreading pool of gore. She buried her face in her hands. Sean pulled her close to him as she silently cried. James watched numbly as both of his classmates shook from the killings they had just performed. He was only dully aware of Firmin bending over and picking up the dropped knife.

The Frenchmen wiped the weapon clean and held it out to Sean. "Votre dame fait le bel art. Elle devrait être fière de la photo qu'elle a peinte aujourd'hui."

Martha looked over her shoulder for what felt like the hundredth time. Even though she couldn't see anyone following, it still felt like eyes were watching her. The weight of her backpack had shifted and was causing more pressure on her left side. She adjusted the strap a little bit more to the right. After a few steps it balanced out on her shoulders.

Everything she could think of for immediate survival was in the pack including extra clothes, packages of dried food, a box of .40 caliber shells for her pistol, and four sixteen-ounce water bottles. After what happened to Scott she knew it was only a matter of time before Brother Abel found an excuse to kill her.

She tried to shake the last image she had of her lover from her mind. Even though he was in her sister's arms and twitching in his death throes it was his eyes that disturbed her the most. They looked confused and frightened, like in his final moments of life he didn't know what was going on or why he was dying.

She felt angry tears start to form. It was all Susan's fault. If her sister could have kept her mouth shut all three of them would be getting out of town now. Or at least she and Scott would be. Her sister had finally fallen under Brother Abel's spell. Like the rest of the damn town. Even though everyone knew he was a psychopath, they were too afraid to stand up to him.

In the last few months she had seen more than a dozen people tortured by that crazy bastard. Keith was getting tired of it. He had talked about holding a meeting, but she wasn't going to stick around long enough to see how that turned out!

She walked down Monroe Street until she came to the Rolla United Methodist Church. She stopped beside a newer black Dodge Ram Quad Cab. Fumbling in her pocket for a few seconds produced the spare key Scott had given her the week before. She glanced in the bed to make sure the three fifty-five gallon gas drums were still secured. She shrugged off her backpack and unlocked the vehicle.

A quick inspection of the back cab yielded two green military surplus containers still buckled in place. She had helped Scott pack them with food and water for the trip. She tossed her heavy backpack into the rear passenger side with a grunt. Leaning down she carefully ran her hand under the seat. She felt the handles of two pistols, an emergency medical kit, and the stock of a shotgun.

She straightened. Looking at lights shining a few blocks over caused a twinge of doubt to knot her stomach. The gravity of travelling alone through a world of monsters slammed into her. Even though it lasted just a moment it was almost enough to make her abandon the plans for escape.

She sensed rather than felt something behind her. Martha almost had her pistol out before a hand clamped down over her mouth. Her arms were wrestled behind her. She tried to pull away, but couldn't break the vice-like grip that held her arms.

"Settle down. We're not going to hurt you. All we need is some information then we'll let you go." The man's voice was calm and low as it continued, "We're looking for some friends of ours; an overweight man that you captured, an average looking guy that speaks French, and two boys and a girl. Have you seen them?"

She stiffened when he mentioned the fat man. If their friend was lucky, he was already dead. She saw a woman with short, blonde hair walk around the bed of Keith's truck. She was followed by a tall dark-haired man wearing some kind of metal armor. Behind them lumbered a leather wearing man with half of his head shaved.

Matt could feel the woman shaking in his arms. He felt sick to his stomach about causing her so much fear. "I am going to let you go now. Be quiet. If you scream you'll force us to kill you. I don't want that."

Matt felt her tense up for a moment. He hated threatening the woman, but could find no alternative to force her cooperation. He slowly pulled his hand from her mouth. When she didn't make a sound he let go of her arms.

"What's your name?"

"Martha."

Matt nodded his head. "Okay, Martha. Where do they have my friend?"

"He was taken to the school. I'm not sure what happens there, but no one comes back out after Brother Abel is done with them."

Ethan took a step toward her. "We have to get there, now!"

"The school is on the corner of Van Buren and Third Avenue. Just take Sixth Avenue down until you get to Van Buren then head north."

Nick snorted. "Awful speedy to sell out aren't ya'? I didn't even get a chance to indulge in a bit of torture."

Martha's face scrunched up in terror. Melissa saw her reaction and slapped the Englishman on his shoulder. "Ignore Nick. His brain doesn't work like the rest of ours. We were never going to hurt you. My name's Melissa and this is Ethan. Matt's the guy behind you."

Martha forced herself to relax. She wanted to get away from the crazed pastor and make her own way in the world. If these were the kind of people out there she may as well start now. "I haven't seen any of your other friends though. If they were caught, they would be held in the intersection with the wooden stage. I am trying to get the hell out of here and away from that crazy old man. He's a monster."

Matt and the others exchanged glances. The former Marine nodded his head. "Nick and I saw what happened to your friend. I'm sorry."

The stranger sounded sincere. Scott's fate resurfaced in her mind. She could feel her stomach knotting up again. Her face felt warm. She couldn't stop the sudden outburst of tears. The men stared at her uncomfortably.

Melissa rushed to her side without any hesitation. She pulled the sobbing woman close in a gentle hug. "Nick told us what happened. It sounded terrible!"

"This truck is his. We were going to leave. We had it all packed and ready to go and then… then—" Martha's words were lost in her tears.

Melissa continued to hold her as she cried. The tender-hearted woman patted her back and rocked slowly back and forth with her. Matt took a more pragmatic approach. Nodding at Ethan and Nick he pointed in the bed of the truck. As his friends checked out that location he took a quick inventory of what was in the cab.

Nick let out a low whistle. "Mate! They're set with enough petrol to hit fucking Mars!"

Ethan's soft voice added, "There's three fifty-five gallon drums back here. We popped one open and it's gas. If the other two are fuel we can make it across the country."

Martha sniffled. "One's filled with water. Scott insisted on it."

Matt put a hand on the grieving woman's shoulder. "Scott was a smart man. It's a good thing you two got all of this together."

Matt looked at the truck again. It would be a tight fit, but he believed they could all find a seat. A few would have to ride in the bed. If they had enough layers of clothing and some extra blankets they shouldn't freeze.

Nick and Matt exchanged glances. The Englishman looked down from the bed of the truck and nodded at the American. Ethan looked in the direction of the school. Melissa finally released Martha from her hug. The sobbing woman wiped her eyes with the back of her hand.

Matt took a deep breath. "Martha, let me run an idea by you…"

"For it was not an enemy that reproached me; then I could have borne it: neither was it he that hated me that did magnify himself against me; then I would have hid myself from him: but it was thou, a man mine equal, my guide, and mine acquaintance. We took sweet counsel together, and walked unto the house of God in company."

Psalm 55:12 -14

IF WISHES WERE HORSES

A series of screams erupted from behind the double doors. Sean and James shifted on their feet impatiently while Firmin tried key after key on the lock. His hands and arms were covered in blood from the search he had administered on the three bodies to retrieve them. Firmin shrugged helplessly at the kids. He dropped the last of the key rings he had found on the floor. None of them had fit the lock. He took four steps to the side and pointed at Sean's 12 Gauge.

The younger boy levelled the shotgun even with the keyhole on the double door. James held his AK-47 tightly against his shoulder. Firmin sighed and drew his pistol. Elizabeth leaned against the wall of the hallway shaking and looking away from the grisly scene she helped create.

James nodded at Sean. They couldn't waste any more time. Their friend needed them. The foreigner and two boys tensed. *BOOM!* The shotgun blast bounced off the walls and echoed throughout the school. Firmin took a quick step toward the door and flung his leg in front of him. The bottom of his foot knocked the doors open. Not losing any momentum he rushed down the stairs.

James scrambled in right behind the Frenchmen. He held the assault rifle's barrel down and to the left as he descended the stairs. Sean racked another shell into the chamber before charging after his friends.

Firmin couldn't fully take in the scenario that filled his eyes as he entered the basement. An older man dressed like a Catholic priest stood over Justin holding a bloody scalpel. His friend was chained to a table. Blood was flowing from a large section of his stomach where the outer layer of his skin had been cut, peeled back, and pinned to the table. A small table with a dried blood spotted sheet covered something a few feet away. The priest looked up at him in surprise. The Frenchman took quick aim and pulled the trigger on his pistol several times.

The man's body jerked as hot lead ripped into him. James's AK-47 spat out more rounds once the kid cleared the final step to the basement. The higher caliber shells threw the torturer backwards. The body crashed into shelves knocking them over into one another. The gore-filled tanks shattered and spilled their contents. The stench of sulfur and decay nearly stole the breath from their lungs.

Machines became soaked in visceral fluids as some containers exploded from stray shots and blow through. A few popped and buzzed before error messages were displayed. In the fraction of a second the floor was covered in blood and organs. Some of the body parts connected to operating machines flopped and scurried around. Heads of all sizes gaped at the intruders from the floor. Many blinked at their sudden freedom. Others panted to draw air into lungs that were no longer attached. Some snapped loose from the tubes that pumped blood into them. These rapidly bit at anything that came close, but became still after a few seconds.

Sean's mouth hung open for a second when he saw the carnage. The shackled man's continued whimpers snapped him to action. In a few strides he was next to his friend. Justin's eyes were wide and glassy. He stared up at him from the table. He blinked several times before his eyes rolled up into his head. Justin convulsed a few times before laying still. Sean started pulling the pins out that held his friend's flayed skin to the table.

James darted to where Brother Abel had fallen. The old man's body was covered in blood. A large, severed hand with tubes shoved into it was clutching at a glass shard protruding from his chest. The priest's own hands were limp at his sides. James stared at the wriggling fingers of the hand in disgust. He felt a strong grip on his left shoulder as Firmin pushed him aside.

The Frenchman hastily pawed through pockets until he found a set of keys. Rushing to Justin's side he tried a few on the shackles holding him until one caused them to click open. He moved around to do the next one, but froze when he saw movement under the red splattered sheet. Reaching out he yanked the covering off.

Firmin's face went slack. His breathing grew heavy. He felt someone prying the keys away from his left hand. He ignored it all. Staring back at him was the most beautiful thing he had ever seen. He gently reached out and stroked the cheek of the freakishly large head. It twisted toward his hand sharply and bit down. Drool dripped from a confused grin on the smaller head.

The Frenchman barely pulled his hand back in time to avoid the attack. A smile spread across his face. He laughed. He dully heard James screaming his name. He stepped behind the edge of the table where the heads were. He ran his hands through both sets of hair. He laughed louder when the little head closed its eyes and licked its lips.

A leg was flexing on the ground next to him. Without thinking he knelt down and picked it up. The additional tension on the tubes pulled them from the machine they were attached to. The limb jerked violently. Firmin clutched it next to his heart. In his immediate vicinity were three torsos from the larger creatures. He also noticed another slender arm. The beauty all around him brought tears to his eyes.

He heard James yelling from the top of the staircase. He only vaguely recognized the voice, but the meaning of the plea was lost on him. He didn't care. He was happy. He was happier than he could ever remember. He couldn't stop the bursts of joyous laughter erupting out of him like a fountain of blood from one of his victims.

James yanked the keys away from Firmin. He cringed when he saw the look on the foreigner's face. He couldn't quite explain what it was, but it seemed a mixture of joy and lust. James finished with the last set of shackles holding Justin to the table. Sean pulled the skin back onto Justin's stomach. The younger boy stripped off his shirt and used it as a makeshift bandage to staunch the flow of blood from the surgical wound.

"Firmin! Firmin!" James shouted as he kicked body parts out of his way, "We need you! Help us carry Justin!"

Sean slid an arm behind Justin's shoulder. "Get your hand under him! Firmin what are you doing?"

James locked his arm under his friend's other shoulder. Together the two boys wrestled him off the table. Both of them grunted when Justin's full weight fell across their bodies. A hand crawling along the floor brushed up against Sean's leg. He tried blocking the surreal feeling from his mind.

Half-carrying and half-dragging Justin the two kids made it to the stairs. Firmin's laughter flooded the basement. The boys glanced back at their friend. He held a still twitching severed leg close to his chest. Tears were flowing from his face as he looked around at all the dismembered bodies.

"He's lost his shit! James! Firmin's lost his shit!"

"We can't do anything about it right now! We need to get Justin back to the others!"

"We aren't going to make it up the stairs like this. Grab his feet!"

James knelt down. He grabbed the unconscious man's legs and stood. Sean struggled with the weight of his torso for a moment, but got it under control once James was standing straight again. Justin's flayed skin peeled back from his left side. The fresh tear immediately began seeping blood. With strength born from fear the two boys lumbered up the stairs.

As they cleared the top James called down, "We'll be back for you!"

Continuing laughter was the only response he got.

"God damn it! Pull yourself together! Fucking help us!"

"Don't yell at her!"

"Sean, if YOU don't start yelling at her I'm going to beat your ass! She's useless right now!"

If Elizabeth heard the exchange she made no move to help them carry Justin. The young woman was still facing away from the three dead men. She sat in the middle of the hall slowly rocking back and forth.

James grunted while adjusting the former pastor's legs in his grasp. "We can't carry her and Justin. She needs to get off her ass!"

"One second! Let me think! Put him down."

"Why in the hell should we—"

"Put him down! I have an idea."

James choked down an angry response. Fighting with Sean would only cause more issues they wouldn't have time to fix. Reluctantly the older boy followed Sean's lead and gently laid Justin on the ground.

"Stay with her. I'll be right back!"

Sean bolted down the hall and disappeared around a corner. James stepped in front of Elizabeth. He shook her roughly by the shoulder a few times. Her head wobbled on her neck. The Z.O.D. sergeant looked down the hall where Sean had dashed. He could hear his friend's footprints fading away.

Looking down at the girl he gritted his teeth. He smacked her across the face. She stopped rocking for a moment, but continued to stare straight ahead of her. He slapped her again. She took a sharp breath. James knelt down next to her. There was a glimmer of recognition in her eyes. She slowly exhaled.

She blinked a few times.

James snapped his fingers. "Can you hear me?"

The girl nodded. A sharp *ting* sounded from the direction Sean had ran.

"Get up! Justin's hurt. You need to walk so me and Sean can carry him."

She slowly started to rock back and forth again. James lashed out. His blow slapped her across her other cheek. She looked up at him in wide-eyed terror.

James held a hand out to her. "On your fucking feet!"

She took his hand. He pulled her up on trembling legs. Footsteps echoed closer to them along with a scraping sound. James pointed his rifle at the intersection. He lowered it when Sean walked backwards around the corner dragging something white. It looked like a busted table top.

When he saw Elizabeth standing he dropped it. Rushing to her side he flung his arms around her. "God it's good to see you up!"

Sean nodded at the white table-looking thing he had been dragging. "It's part of one of those 'smart board' dohickies. I ripped it off the wall and busted it in half. I thought we could put Liz and Justin on it and pull them. Now it can just be for him."

James lifted the board to study it. The thing wasn't light, but with him and Sean pulling it they could get Justin out of town a lot faster. He dropped it. Looking over at Justin he nodded. "Let's get him loaded."

It took a few tries to get the hang of pulling the make-shift stretcher. During their first attempt they lifted it too high and Justin spilled off the back. The second time was much better, but they had to set him down to adjust the straps on their guns. The third time was the charm. Justin gritted his teeth against the noise it made. The grating screech as it was pulled along the hall would present a new problem when they made it outside. They worked their back toward the exit.

They passed an intersection. They could see the doors they had entered the school through about thirty yards away. The doors were standing open and led to a clear street. Elizabeth stopped.

"What's wrong, sweetie?"

The girl turned toward them. Her eyes were wide. Her lips were trembling. "Firmin shut the door when we came in. We're not alone."

Sean and James eased the board down. The emergency lights flickered for a few seconds then went out. All of them held their breath. A faint *click-click-click* tapped out behind them. As one they turned toward the sound. They couldn't see more than a few feet down the darkened hall.

"Elizabeth, help James drag Justin out of here."

"What? Why can't you?"

James tensed. "What are you doing, man?"

Sean bounded down the hall back the way they had just come and rounded the corner of the intersection. "Get them out of here James!"

"Come back!" Elizabeth's voice chased after him down the corridor.

He propelled himself down the hall. He wished he could have had time to explain what his plan was. Unfortunately he had no way of knowing how close the monsters really were to them. He couldn't risk them attacking while Justin was helpless. He hoped they would trust him enough to keep going.

The clicking of nails on concrete intensified behind him. Lights flickered back to life. Soon the thuds of heavy footfalls joined in. Sean knew he was faster than everyone in his class, but he held little faith he could match the demonic beasts giving chase for long. Screeches began accompanying the sounds of pursuit. He knew with a certainty they were now close behind.

He didn't realize just how close until he felt his right leg jerked out from underneath him. He landed face first on the cold floor. He felt a flash of searing pain race across his jaw and nose. Instinctively he flopped over on his back and kicked out. Through watery eyes he could see blurred images tumbling over each other as his assailant fell back into the group.

While shuffling backwards to get away from the creatures he bumped the doorstop on one of the classrooms. The heavy portal started to close. Not seeing an alternative he dove into the room just before it slammed shut.

He vaulted to his feet. Spinning around, Sean slapped the deadbolt in place. A ghoulish young, grey face pressed itself against the small, rectangular windowpane in the door. The visage of the creature alternated between smiling and scowling. It banged the glass a few times with its fist. The thick material spider-webbed out from the center under the blows.

An empty holster greeted his hand as it darted for his 9 mm. He glanced around on the ground looking for the lost pistol. He patted his belt quickly and couldn't feel his knife sheath either. His shotgun was lying next to Justin on the smart board. Coming up short on weapons he groaned when the realization hit him that he was unarmed.

Clunk! Another strike from the beast knocked a small chunk of the wire-mesh glass from the top corner of the window. He heard more creatures outside the door trying to scramble over each other to get to him. Wails filled the room as the twisted children fought each other.

Sean pushed the teacher's desk toward the door. He tipped it over when he got closer. Shoving it tightly next to the frame he wedged it as close as the top of the desk would allow. He raced around the room grabbing chairs and smaller desks. He tossed them on top of each other to add weight to the barricade.

A small, circular desk fan rested against the wall behind where the teacher's desk had been. Sean snatched it up and looped the cord in his hands a few times. It wasn't much of a weapon, but it was better than nothing.

Banging continued on the door. Sean heard more glass hit the floor. So far his makeshift barricade was holding. The windows in the room's exterior were rectangular. He rushed to the nearest one and clicked the latch open. Another groan escaped him when he pulled on it and it came toward him only a little over one-third of the way instead of up. He tried to fit through, but it was too narrow for him.

He tried the next window with the same result. Then the next one. Then a third one. The same result each time… a partially open window he couldn't hope to fit through. Shaking in frustration Sean started pulling drawers out of cabinets. He threw one after another on top of the pile of desks and chairs. All kinds of useless junk was landing near his feet. Pencils, pens, reams of paper, staples… a broken paper cutter.

The blade had been broken off somehow and must have been put in the drawer instead of thrown away. It was an older looking handle, heavy and wooden. The blade was almost two feet long and curved like a katana. Sean snatched it from the ground.

The banging on the door intensified. The remaining glass shattered. He heard the splintering of wood. Soon afterward he heard the deadbolt land with a *thwack* on the floor. He turned around at the sound of his barricade being moved aside by the opening door.

Fan in one hand and broken paper cutter blade in the other, he rushed at the first creeper that came through the desks. Leading with the fan he caught the beast on its chin. It flopped to its side and clutched at its jaw. The second gray-mottled monster met the paper cutter with its forehead. The remaining safety covering of the blade erupted into a hundred shards of plastic from the impact.

The gash didn't go through the creature's skull, but it did cause it to screech in pain and try to hop backwards and away from him. The pile of chairs and desks, along with the other hell-spawn trying to rush in, made escape impossible for the beast. Sean hacked down again catching it along the side of the head, severing an ear. The reek of sulfur and decay assaulted him.

The hell-child shifted tactics. Instead of backing away, it lunged forward. A sharp swipe from its talons opened a wide gash along Sean's neck and upper chest. The cord of the fan slipped from his hand as he grabbed the wound. Outside in the hall he heard a new chorus of wailing. His mind reeled in pain. *They must have smelled my blood!*

His adversary cackled. Sean backpedaled a few feet away and then sprung with the paper cutter. The keen edge of his weapon sliced cleanly through the neck of his foe. Yellow, garish blood sprayed his face. The hell-child pitched sideways onto the floor and flailed. It was quickly replaced by a new one.

Sean couldn't tell how many more there were. It didn't really matter to him anymore. His breathing was already labored. His blood was mingling with that of the creepers on the floor to create sickly orange color. He was losing too much. It was hard for him to stay on his feet. Sensing his weakness, the monster in front of him smiled.

He tried taking a step away from the beast. He was tired. He lost his footing and slipped in the pool of gore. Behind his opponent, another fiend scampered into the room. His ears rang for a moment. He was getting colder. *BANG! BANG! BANG! BAM! BAM! BAM!* The sounds grew louder next to the door. He shut his eyes. The last thing he heard was his barricade tumbling down around him.

A block away from the school Melissa abruptly leaned forward and pointed to the side of a small brick house. "There! Stop! Right there!"

Her outburst nearly caused Matt to run off the road. He stomped on the brake of the truck. Nick was out of the bed and running before the vehicle screeched to a stop. He looked to where she was pointing. Other than clumps of bushes he couldn't see anything. Matt threw the truck in park when Nick came bounding out of the bushes with Justin slumped over his shoulder. Elizabeth and James were in tow. Sean and Firmin were nowhere to be seen. Melissa and Martha bailed out of the truck. Nick stretched their wounded friend out in the back of the cab as best he could.

Once Justin was secured James dashed back toward the school. "Sean and Firmin are still inside with a bunch of monsters! We have to save them!"

"James, Get back here! Ethan, where are you… Nick, stay with… FUCK!" Matt cursed as people scattered. "Elizabeth, hold that dressing as tight as you can to Justin's wound. You ladies wait here and keep the truck running!"

Matt grabbed his AR-15 from the gun rack and bolted after

his friends. Ethan's long strides easily closed the distance between him and James. Soon the lanky man was leading the charge to the school. Nick lumbered along behind the faster pair. He was soon joined by Matt.

The former Marine looked pissed as he barreled past the Englishman. "Wait! We need a plan!"

"Ethan! Stop! Listen to the bloody expert!"

Matt's anger intensified when Ethan rushed inside the building followed a few seconds later by James. "Nick, I'm gonna' kill those fuckin' idiots!"

"Hopefully you'll get a chance to."

Ethan's eyes had trouble adjusting to the lighting inside the school. Wails of demonic lust for flesh permeated the hallways making it difficult to get a bearing on where Sean and Firmin could be. He held the shotgun at his shoulder while he navigated the school. Making his best guess on where the creatures were, he turned right at an intersection. After a few more bounds down the hall he heard heavy banging.

Ethan took off in a run. Rounding the corner of another intersection he plowed through a group of four creepers. The largest of the monsters barely came to his waist. Ethan's momentum flung the creatures to the ground. Stepping on one of their shoulders caused him to lose his footing. He sprawled face forward toward the cold, hard concrete. He let go of his gun as he fell to throw his hands up and catch himself.

He slid along the ground a few feet. His armor shrieked in complaint. He leapt to his feet with mace in hand. One of the gray-skinned devils launched itself at him. His heavy steel mace crushed its skull mid-flight. The other three beasts had scrambled to their feet as well. They spread out. Ethan backed away holding his weapon at the ready. He was so intent on his opponents that he didn't see the classroom door hanging off its hinges.

BLAM! The top half of the smallest zombies head exploded. The remaining two spun around. James's AK-47 blasted more rounds at the beasts as he advanced down the hall. He kept

Ethan far from his line of fire. The Z.O.D. sergeant intentionally shot wide; more interested in keeping their attention on him than doing any real damage. He didn't have the nerve to bring his weapon to bear within five feet of his friend. James look of shock was completely genuine when a shot rang out behind him. The left side of the monster's head closest to Ethan instantly disintegrated in a cloud of yellowish ooze.

The remaining beast sprang backwards. Matt fired two more times, but the speed of the monster saved its life. It bolted down the hall and around the corner in retreat. Nick gave chase. He slid to a halt as he passed the destroyed door when his mind registered two more of the imps inside the classroom.

With a speed he never thought himself possible of Nick levelled the barrel of his shotgun at the creatures standing over Sean. "Hey! Fuckers!"

The hell-children looked at him in unison. The displaced Englishman fired, racked a shell, and fired again. Both blasts belched flame and shot at the doomed beasts. In the blink of an eye they both crumpled and lay still next to the unconscious teenager.

Nick entered the room in furious desperation. He pulled, kicked, and flipped chairs and desks out of his way to get to the kid's side. Ethan appeared next to him. Together they bulldozed through the rest of the barricade. Nick's face twisted into a grimace when he saw the ghastly wound Sean had suffered.

Nick pressed his hands over the gashes. "Bandages! Sean's right proper fucked! We need fucking bandages right fucking now!"

James ran into the room pulling his coat off. He quickly shrugged off his shirt and tossed it to Nick. Matt grabbed Ethan and turned him towards him.

"Go get the truck!"

Ethan nodded and with one last look at Sean galloped toward the exit. James pulled his coat back on. He stared down with worry at his friend.

Matt shook James's shoulder. "James! Where's Firmin?"

"He's in the basement! Take a right when you walk out the door and then a left at the next intersection."

Matt nodded. "Get Sean outside and in the truck when it gets here. Those shots are gonna' bring everyone running. I'm grabbing Firmin and then I'll meet you! Nick, I'm counting on you!"

The Englishman's face was grim when he looked up. "I can't even take care of my fucking self!"

Matt was already halfway out the door. "You're in charge!"

James knelt down next to Sean. "It looks bad doesn't it?"

Nick blinked at him. "It sure ain't a fucking stubbed toe."

Matt stopped dead in his tracks after he turned left at the intersection. The hallway in front of him was filled with monstrosities of all sizes. He ducked around the corner and put his back flat against the wall. He took a slow deep breath. None of the beasts were making a sound.

He crept back the way he came. He took each step as lightly as he could. He looked over his shoulder every few seconds. He froze when one of the oversized zombies turned the corner. The creature stopped. Eyes that were much too small for such a large head regarded him curiously for a moment. It snorted at him, then turned and walked back around the corner.

Matt gulped in disbelief. Not wanting to push his luck he hurried toward the exit. Noticing a rolling gate on the ceiling of the hall, he pulled it shut behind him. At the next intersection he found another one. He slid it closed as well.

"Why hello there stranger!"

He was just about to walk out the door when the familiar voice sent chills along his spine. He couldn't believe his ears. He turned around. His eyes held the same disbelief. Father Murray was standing at the first closed gate. He was wearing priest vestments, right down to the white clerical collar. Surrounding him were the nightmarish rulers of the apocalypse.

Grey-skinned brutes that almost touched the roof of the hall with their heads stood elbow to elbow with smaller, thinner demonic creatures. Pale as a drained corpse they looked more human than any of the others, but their twisted grins were filled with teeth just as sharp. Creepers weaved in and out from between the legs of the other beasts.

Matt gaped at him. "You're alive!"

Thomas smiled. "That's more than I can say about you in a minute."

"Where's Firmin? Let him go. Everyone walks away. No fighting."

"Can't do that. Hell, I won't do that," Thomas laughed. "Besides, he's happy right where he is. He's found his place in the new world!"

"His place is with us!"

The laughter fled from Father Murray's voice. "You don't know how wrong you are about that."

Matt had no idea how the man could stand in the center of such hellish monsters without being ripped to shreds. Father Murray seemed confident in his own safety. So much so that Matt held no doubt that the monsters were under his control somehow. He weighed his options. He knew he could get one or two shots off at Thomas before the beasts next to the priest tore through the feeble metal gate.

Matt's mind was doing somersaults. "What happened to you?"

A creeper stood at his side. The fallen priest absently rested his hand on the creature's head. When he saw Matt cringe, he smiled at him. "I met a goddess. She chose me to be her consort."

"Are you serious?"

Father Murray's smile grew wider. "Not that it makes any difference to me what you think, but yes. I'm deadly serious. Of course I could be persuaded to let you and your other friends go."

"How can I do that?"

"Leave Sean behind. Set him on the sidewalk and drive away. He won't live much longer anyway. Not with his neck laid open like it is."

"How did you—"

"Know? Because young Lewis here showed me everything he just saw." Laughing, Thomas ruffled the hair of the creature his hand rested on.

Matt couldn't suppress a shudder. The kids talked about a friend they had named Lewis a lot. Deep in his heart he knew that the beast next to the twisted priest was the same person. The realization brought another dark thought to him. How did Thomas communicate with these things?

"What's your answer?" All jovialness was gone from Father Murray.

Matt spun on his heels. He heard several loud *twangs* as the metal gate was ripped apart. He was out the door when the second gate came crashing down. Above the roar of the monsters chasing him he could hear Thomas laughing.

The former Marine caught a lucky break as he fled from the school. Ethan was pulling up on the lawn. Nick was in the bed of the truck with James. Both of their AK-47's blasted a steady stream of hot lead at the pursuing beasts. Inside the cab Melissa took aim with her .308. Her shot downed a pale-skinned one.

Matt vaulted over the side of the bed. He landed on top of James sending them both sprawling. Matt's rifle and the kid's AK-47 were flung from their hands and off the other side of the truck bed.

Nick screamed, "Go! Go! Go!"

Ethan gunned the engine. The powerful motor caused the tires to rip sections of lawn from the ground. It sprayed the debris behind the vehicle into the faces of the beasts as the truck sped off. Nick continued to fire behind them at the mass of creatures. James and Matt could only watch helplessly as the Englishman's shots collided with a large brute that led the pack. Chunks of fetid flesh were torn from the monster, but it kept up its pace. The smallest creeper any of them had ever seen was clinging to the larger one's shoulder. Its screeching outweighed the sounds of gunfire and roars of the other fiends.

The truck lurched hard to the side as Ethan sharply turned left onto First Avenue. They saw people rushing toward the school. Most of them were carrying guns, but some had bats and other hand-held weapons. Cries erupted from the mob of people when they caught sight of the horde of monsters. Shots were fired. A lot of the beasts veered off and stormed into the townsfolk.

As they raced off into the night gunfire continued behind them for a short time. Then the only sound they heard was the roar of the engine. Nick set his weapon down. He leaned against the tailgate, wiped his eyes, and rested his chin in his right hand. Matt nodded at him, then tapped on the back glass of the truck. Ethan slowed to a stop.

The lanky driver rolled his window down and stuck his head out. "What's up?"

"How's Justin and Sean?"

"Justin's sleeping and his bleedings stopped. Sean is… I don't know. He lost a lot of blood and his breathing sounds weak."

Martha spoke from the center seat, "I got the kid's wounds packed. They look bad. I don't even know how he's still alive."

Melissa called out from the other side of the cab, "Elizabeth passed out. I put her on the floor next to Sean."

Matt nodded. "Okay. Get us out of here, Ethan. Stay on this road. We'll stop when he hit Oklahoma and settle on a plan."

"Okay."

Ethan eased his foot down on the gas. James pulled his coat tighter to his shirtless chest. Nick looked out into the darkness feeling numb. Miles went by before the Englishman spoke.

"Frenchy's dead?"

Matt shook his head. "I don't know, but for his sake I hope he is."

Nick and James both looked at Matt.

The former Marine looked gravely at each of them. "The good Father Murray is alive and well and somehow in control of those things."

James sucked in his breath. "Well, at least all the good guys are in the same truck this time."

Nick rolled his eyes and turned back to the darkness. "Look on the bright side, mate. This will spark a whole new resurgence of priest jokes. How's this one sound? A priest and a zombie walk into a bar…"

EPILOGUE

Father Murray watched the tail lights of the truck disappear down Highway 56. He was angry that they had gotten away, but his emotions were tempered with confidence that he would catch up to them soon enough. Gunfire blared across town. He was sure that his consort's pets could easily handle any remaining resistance.

He smelled sulfur a moment before the shadow fell across him. He turned and smiled at the source. "A beautiful sound isn't it?"

Brother Abel's eyebrows were narrowed dangerously low on his brow. "She didn't have to kill them all."

"Only a few of them are going to die. The rest will be turned into soldiers for her army. They'll be bitten and mauled, but will survive."

The old man straightened his bullet ridden and blood laden cassock. "What does she want us to do now?"

"For the next week we collect bodies. After that I don't know. She said she'd send Lewis with orders."

"Why doesn't she use the larger ones? They run faster."

"Why does she do anything? I'm not going to ask questions."

Silence hung in the air for a few moments before Brother Abel asked, "So I have the virus now?"

Thomas smirked at him. "Sorry man. That's the only explanation of how you survived all the gunshots, not to mention that large shank you got from behind. God knows you got covered in enough of their blood. I think you'll start changing soon."

Brother Abel glared back at the fallen priest. "At least I won't have to put up with your smug face for long then. You're bedding her now, eh?"

The fallen priest smirked at the older man. "She's hot."

Brother Abel returned the smirk with a warm smile. "Sex with her has a way of changing a man."

Thomas nodded gravely. "Do you think our new friend is having fun yet?"

The ghost of a smile crept across the doomed surgeons face. "I think he is in Heaven."

The walls of the basement, the gunfire, thoughts of his friends… everything faded away from him. He looked down at his creation. Firmin smiled. Tears rolled from his eyes as he took in the magnificence of his work. He cupped his mouth in his hands to keep from laughing.

Four sets of arms wiggled fingers. He had been worried at first that it wouldn't work, but after a few hours it seemed that the magic brought the additional arms he had sewn to the torso to life. All of his dreams were coming true. He could mix and match flesh to his heart's content.

What made him cry though was watching the movements his children made. From walking on four legs, to now being able to use four arms… his spirit soared as they flourished. He wiped his eyes to clear his vision. He absently started whistling as he went to work on his next project.

Standing at the bottom of the stairs, Father Murray nudged Brother Abel. "How does it work?"

"The virus is amazing. As long as blood can be circulated even a little bit it starts fusing with the host."

Thomas smiled. "So the possibilities are endless?"

"Yes."

Firmin emitted a shriek of pure excitement and joy as his newest child leapt from the table. He hugged the large brute as best he could, his arms too short to wrap around the oversized torso. The Frenchman hummed as he walked along the rows of newly filled tanks.

Father Murray chuckled. "I think you're right. He's having the time of his life."

ABOUT THE AUTHOR

Edward Gehlert has always been fascinated by the power of the written word. From a young age he has been carried along on magical journeys which were weaved by skilled storytellers and his dream was to one day join them.

He started his career in the publishing industry in 2000 as a copy editor. Since that time he has written more than thirty books. These works were military base guides, welcome guides, and business guides as well as informational booklets for the Social Security Administration and National Institutes of Health. He has also written countless articles that have appeared in various media outlets.

In 2014 his first novel, *Dark Harvest*, was released by New Babel Books. Set in Shane Moore's *Apocalypse of Enoch* world, the story follows an orphan and his group of friends as the end of the world as they know it comes to an end. This is his second novel and is a continuation of the *Children of Enoch* series.

He recently accepted a job as the Editorial Manager for Happy Duck Publishing after having held the same title at F&M Publishing for the past seven years. He invites everyone to visit him at his author page on Facebook (www.facebook.com/AuthorEdwardGehlert) and drop a message.

Edward currently resides in Mid-Missouri with his wife, Eva, and son, Wayde.

Check out these other great titles from New Babel Books:

The Apocalypse of Enoch Series
"Rapture"
"Scourge"
"Desolation"

Abyss Walker titles

Core Series
"The Plea of Apollisian"
"The Trial of Innocence"
"Darrion-Quieness"
"Death of Kings"
"Tides of Winter"
"Return of the Father"

The Wererat's Tale Series
"The Wererat's Tale-Of Rats and Men"
"The Wererat's Tale-Ring of the Nonul"
"The Wererat's Tale-The Collar of Perdition"

White Wraith Series
"White Wraith-The Escape"
"White Wraith-Lock of Requ"
"White Wraith-Malestrom Serpents"

For additional NBB titles, visit: www.newbabelbooks.com

Go to www.Zod001.com and Join for Free!

www.ingramcontent.com/pod-product-compliance
Lightning Source LLC
Chambersburg PA
CBHW070124260626
47160CB00004B/1618